# Purrfectly Trapped

## A MAVERICK PRIDE TALE

### THE MAVERICK PRIDE TALES
### BOOK THREE

## C.D. GORRI

Purrfectly Trapped:
A Maverick Pride Tale #3
by C.D. Gorri
Edited by T. P. of BookNookNuts

Copyright 2020 C.D. Gorri

*For Patricia, Tammy, and Julia! You are the purrfect writing buddies and cheerleaders for a gal like me! Love ya to bits! Xoxo*

BLURB

**Gretchen has spent a lifetime searching for love. Now the only man she wants thinks he's a Tiger!**

*Cut It Out* is open for business! Moving to Maverick Point for affordable rents and to be near her bestie was a no brainer. But Gretchen had no idea her first client was going to be six and a half feet of gorgeousness.

Hot or not, the man is desperate for a trim and shave. Not a problem. Well, it wouldn't be, if she could stop staring at all those muscles and focus on his unkempt locks instead. But a girl's got needs…

Reg has been trying to make amends for past mistakes, neglecting other things in the process. *Like his hair and beard.* Not good for a Tiger chosen to guard the precious Nari of the Maverick Pride.

When Uncle Uzzi comes for a consultation, he orders the Tiger to get his overly furry butt to the new salon pronto. Reg isn't too convinced the Witch knows what he's doing, until the second he enters the salon and scents his mate.

There is just one problem. The sassy stylist doesn't know a thing about Shifters. Can Reg convince her to be his? He has no choice.

This Tiger won't rest until the fiery little human is purrfectly trapped.

# Welcome to Uncle Uzzi's Magical Matchmaking Service!

Uzzi Stregovich has been working with the supernatural community for decades, offering his Magical Matchmaking Service to anyone with an open mind and loyal heart.

Finding true mates was what the old Witch did best, and the Tigers of Maverick Point, New Jersey had been the focus of his last two successes.

Mail was piling up, but Uzzi could not seem to think about anything other than the Tiger Pride. After successfully matching the Neta up with his beautiful Nari, followed by the Bear Shifter and his lovely she-Tiger, Uzzi was feeling quite chuffed about himself.

"Who will be next?" the Witch wondered as his magic buzzed and hummed.

A blessing, that was what his *liebling* had called Uzzi's particular talents for sniffing out mates, though it was the Shifters he catered to who did the actual sniffing.

"A joke," he whispered, knowing how his dearly departed wife would have rolled her pretty eyes at his humor.

But Uzzi always knew when the makings of true love were afoot, and he relished the adventure that was about to start!

*Ah yes, sometimes a little tough love is needed before we start the fun.*

**H**mm. *What to do first?*

Uzzi Stregovich, or Uncle Uzzi as his clients lovingly referred to the elderly Witch, sat at his desk contemplating his next case. He had so much work at the moment, but for some reason he kept coming back to one particular group of pussies.

Snickering at his own clever use of the term, he blushed as his gaze raked across the photo of his liebling on their wedding day.

Oh, she'd been the picture of beauty and grace. Too good for a crass Witch like him, but he'd loved her. How he'd loved her! Still did, in fact. His Betty was a treasure unlike any other.

A descendent of the goddess of love herself, as

some in his family tree had declared and often, Uncle Uzzi was gifted with a certain talent for bringing fated mates together. It was difficult at times, especially when his clients proved ornery, or even worse, clueless.

His mind wandered back to that Tiger Shifter Pride out in Burlington County, New Jersey. They were a handful, but he absolutely adored them. Especially the Neta and Nari of the Maverick Pride.

Elissa and Hunter were like honorary family to Uncle Uzzi, and they felt the same about him. He knew from the frequency with which they wrote, and the fact that, being a Witch whose talent involved matters of the heart, Uzzi had a nose for these things. No wonder he couldn't stop thinking about them.

Settling in with a delicious cup of tea and one of the special double chocolate fudge cookies his housekeeper had baked, Uncle Uzzi scanned his runes and muttered a spell.

*Yes. That is the one.*

He reached for the confounded *vunderbox*, or cell phone, as they were called and opened his electronic mail thingamajig. This is the note he'd been searching for, he thought with a crunch of the delicious cookie. Uncle Uzzi clicked on the message, double checking the name of the sender first.

*Gretchen. Gretchen? Ah, yes!*

She was a close friend of Elissa's, the Nari of the Maverick Pride. He skimmed the email quickly at first, then re-read the missive slowly. A small smile teased at the corner of his lips, and Uncle Uzzi chuckled to himself. This was going to be perfect.

*Dear Uncle Uzzi,*

*My name is Gretchen Kaepernick. You might have heard about me, you see, I'm Elissa Phoenix-Maverick's former roommate. Well, I suppose I should just get right to it.*

*As it happens, I am moving to Maverick Point to take over the lease on the old hair salon from Mrs. Bowers. The owner is giving me the space with an option to buy at the end of one year.*

*I've always wanted to run my own salon, and this is a great opportunity. Everything is in perfect order. I just have a few changes in furniture and appliances, and bam, I am ready to move in. I should have it all up and running just in time for spring haircuts and prom season! LOL.*

*Now, to get to the real point of this email. You see, I haven't had much luck with men in like forever, and I was wondering if you could arrange for me to meet a nice one? I am a bigger than average girl, and I don't want to settle for anyone who thinks they can change me into something else.*

*Pardon my frankness, but I'm not looking for a dietician or a gym instructor. I'm looking for a man who can handle and appreciate all this goodness.*

*It is true, I can come on a bit strong and, okay, well, I'm just plain blunt when it comes to how I feel about my size and looks. They just aren't up for discussion.*

*Praise—yes. Hints about how I can look better--- hard no.*

*Elissa tells me I am too frank, but I can't help it. I turn all my dates away with talk of wanting a future and a family someday. But it's the truth, Uncle Uzzi. It's what I want.*

*You did such a wonderful job with helping Elissa, I wanted to contact you about maybe helping me find my own happily-ever-after?*

*So, what do you think? Can you help me, Uncle Uzzi?*

*Thank you for your consideration,*

*Gretchen K.*

Uncle Uzzi clicked the button on the tiny box in his hand, turning the screen black.

*Well, how about that?* He thought with a full grin on his face.

Things were certainly going to heat up in the Pride with this feisty little human moving in, and wouldn't you know it, Uncle Uzzi had just the Tiger in mind for the sassy female.

He stirred his tea, foregoing more sugar, and began to make plans. Plotting was ninety percent of any good matchmaker's bag of tricks. And Uncle Uzzi was the best, to hear others tell it.

There was only one slight issue to be concerned with. Would this little normal, who had no knowledge of Shifters, be as open as her friend was to the possibility of being mated to a man who also turned into a beast?

"Gretchen Kaepernick, I have got just the man for you," Uzzi said to himself while sifting through the notes he'd taken on each member of the Pride.

His magic began to tingle, little lightning bolts of blue and gold sparking from his fingertips as he scanned names and recalled faces.

Suddenly, Uncle Uzzi stopped skimming. His blue eyes were blazing as he found the name he'd been looking for.

*Ah, yes.*

This was the one. The Tiger who was meant for the beauty salon owner. He chuckled to himself as he recalled the man's face. True, he had issues with the pride, but he'd been young and naive. The Neta had assured Uzzi, this man was as good as they came. He would not represent him otherwise.

That said, it was quite possible Gretchen would have a mate before the end of the week.

*Poor little pussy,* Uzzi thought again, snorting at his joke. The Tiger had no idea what he was in for, Uncle Uzzi chuckled and sipped his tea.

*Sorry, liebling, I will try to behave.*

But his blue eyes were sparkling with mischief as he called to make an appointment with his driver for the following day. They had a trip to take.

B*ack in Maverick Point...*

"Well, what did you learn?" Hunter Maverick, Neta of the Maverick Pride stood before his most trusted men and waited for them to report their findings.

"The streak couldn't have been working alone, Neta," Brayden, his Beta and also the only Black Bear Shifter in the Pride, spoke first.

"They knew exactly where to find the women at their most vulnerable, without any of us there to protect them," Lance added.

He was the youngest Tiger in the Neta's guard of elite warriors. He'd chosen only the best, and Lance, though young, was already deadly with claws and fang. He was a valuable member of Hunter's Guard and the Maverick Pride.

"I suppose we are lucky they grossly underestimated our females then," Reg said with a grin.

"Jessica and Kylie dished out quite the ass kicking," Brayden grinned.

"The Nari was placed in danger because of these rogues. As was my sister, and a new member of our Pride. Ass kicking or not, I won't risk them again. None of us will rest until we have all the answers," Hunter's voice was low and deep with his beast.

A good and strong leader, the Maverick Pride Neta clearly did not find anything about the recent occurrences amusing, least of all the fact that his pregnant mate had been in danger.

"Of course," Brayden said, baring his throat in reverence to the male.

"Back to the point at hand, Neta," Mikey, their healer, said, looking at Hunter before quickly averting his gaze.

Hunter's hackles had been raised, and he began to growl deep and low in his chest, using that special infrasonic pitch that let others in the area know a true predator was close. Prey froze when they heard that sound, and though Mikey and the other members of the Guard were not his prey, they all bowed and bared their throats to the most dominant Shifter in the room.

As the Neta, Hunter was the strongest of them all, but that wasn't the reason his men submitted to him. Strong was one thing, just was another. And Hunter Maverick was the most fair and just Tiger in all of Maverick Point.

His Shifters trusted him to protect, guide, and honor the code they lived by. The Maverick Pride was unique in that the men and women were offered voices in the form of discussions, much like a town meeting.

They called it a *circle*, and all were welcome to participate. Hunter refused to run roughshod over his Pride mates. Loyalty was hard won by Alphas who used their powers to control, Hunter refused to do that. They lived by an honor code, and no one remained who was disloyal to the Pride.

"At the last circle, I noticed many of our younger Tigers did not attend," Mikey continued.

"What do you mean?" Hunter asked.

"I just think we need to keep an eye out. Maybe at the next run?"

"Good idea. Let's keep searching for answers then. Our friend on the Shifter Council, Dakota

Miles, has agreed with our supposition that the streak had help to carry out their plans. Help from someone other than Blake," he said and allowed that unpleasant thought to settle amongst his Guard.

"That means there is a traitor in our midst," he continued, and Hunter's teal gaze landed on each and every one of his trusted men. "I want you all to be on the lookout for any signs that could lead to this person or persons. No one is above consideration. The safety of our Pride and our cherished females is of the utmost importance."

"Yes, Neta," the males responded.

"Alright. You are all dismissed, but not you Reg. I need a word."

The others filed out of the office and Reg stood in the room, waiting while the other men departed. His heart thudded at being singled out, but he understood.

A heavy weight settled on his chest. But he deserved any and all discomfort it afforded. After all, Reg had disgraced himself, threatening his standing within the Pride. He had betrayed Hunter once.

Perhaps his leader believed him capable of doing so again. Shame filled him at the thought, but he held his head high. Reg was not the traitor. Not this time. He had proved himself, and would continue to do so, with unending loyalty to his Neta and the Nari, and to the Pride as a whole.

That was the vow he'd made to the ruling couple, to his Pride mates, and to himself.

"Reg," Hunter said, cocking his head and looking at the younger Tiger.

What did he see when he looked at him? Reg wondered.

*A betrayer? Just another muscled up meathead? Or a loyal Guard?*

"I need to ask something of you."

"Yes, Neta? I will do anything to prove myself worthy of my position here---"

"You have done that, son," Hunter said, gently grasping Reg's shoulder and giving him a small squeeze. Physical contact was a part of life amongst Pride mates, and to be handled thus by his Neta was both reassuring and an honor.

"What I need," the Neta continued, "is for you to make sure the Nari is protected at all times, especially when she leaves the Pride House."

Hunter's Tiger was riding him hard, giving a bite and urgency to his tone that had Reg's knees buckling. The Neta's authority shone in the power of his Alpha voice, and it pressed down on the younger male until he could hardly stand.

It was a struggle, for sure. But Reg understood. A mated Tiger was a protective beast unlike any other. Now that he'd had a good wake up call, he was thrilled the leader of the Maverick Pride had found his fated mate.

It gave him hope. Maybe someday, if the gods were kind, Reg would find his own true and fated someone. That person who the universe had created just for him. The other half to his soul.

*Please gods.*

But he was not all that optimistic he deserved one. After all, he was partially responsible for the damage that asshole Blake had tried to inflict on Hunter and Elissa.

"Yes, Neta," he grunted under the pressure, vowing again and always to protect the Nari, and their Pride with his very life.

"Sorry about that," Hunter said, backing off his Alpha voice as he wiped a hand over his face. "My Tiger is a bit testy these days."

"I understand, Neta. I would be too if I were expecting a cub."

"Yes," the man replied, grinning widely. "What Tiger wouldn't be? I want to feel joyful, to share in the bliss my mate should be basking in at this blessed time, but this whole thing is a mess. It has me wanting to interrogate every single one of our Pride members."

"I understand," Reg replied. Hell. He would be that way too.

"But I don't want to act the tyrant, Reg. While we are still investigating, there is still reason to believe danger is lurking out there. I need to know Elissa is safe when she is not with me."

"I swear it, Neta, I will protect her with my life-"

"Good. By trusting you with my mate and heir, I am trusting you with my life, Reg. Keep her safe. Keep her home if you can. That way we can all protect her."

"I will try, but you know how the Nari is. She does not want to stay still. The young one has her restless," Reg replied, a knowing grin on his face.

Elissa was a tough one. The perfect match for the Neta in every way. She'd come to him a full human, but after their mating had been blessed by the Fates with the *Puspa*. She was now a fierce Tiger, beautiful and powerful in her own right.

"I know, that is why I am counting on you to watch her when I am not there. I am sending you a copy of her schedule for the week. It should help with arranging security and guards," Hunter said.

"Yes, Neta," Reg returned.

He left the Neta's office and headed to his room. Glancing over the schedule he'd just received, he noted the next day was going to be a busy one. The Nari was expecting a guest. The elderly Witch was quickly becoming a regular at the Pride House. Uzzi Stregovich had introduced the ruling couple and was treated like family ever since.

Reg had no opinion on the man either way. He was fair, he supposed, and kind, and that was good enough for the Tiger. He scrolled ahead and saw the Nari had some appointments over the following weeks, but not much. Who knew part of being a guard would mean he'd have administration duties as well?

He shrugged and tugged off his shirt. Oh well, at least they would be staying at the Pride House for the most part.

Maybe he could tempt the Nari into staying and practicing the authentic *cioppino* recipe he'd scrounged up for her after emailing some distant cousins who lived off the Amalfi coast. He could have a fresh fish delivery brought to the house for the delicious Italian fish stew.

Elissa was a chef. She loved to cook. And as it happened, the Tigers of the Pride loved to eat. Reg included.

It was a perfect plan to keep her safe and his Neta happy. Then maybe everyone could stop looking at him as if he were still a traitor. Reg knew the men didn't think he was aware of it, but he knew. The second those words had left Hunter's mouth that they were looking for someone who'd betrayed them, Reg had felt their eyes on him. No matter that he'd apologized and tried everything he could to make up for his actions, they still doubted him.

It hurt Reg that they still did not trust his motives. But he wasn't a child. He was a Tiger. And he would prove himself by being devoted to his job and Pride duties.

They would trust him again. All of them.

*I swear I will do everything I can to make it right.*

# Chapter One

"That's the last one!" Gretchen shouted, stretching her sore back.

"*Ohmygawd, Gretch!* I don't know what you were worried about," Elissa huffed, sitting down on a plastic covered chair, and rubbing her protruding belly.

The shipment of bright orange, faux leather chairs had only just been delivered, and Gretchen had yet to unwrap them all.

"Do you need a bottle of water?" Gretchen asked her bestie. She hardly recognized Lissa these days.

Her former roommate was practically glowing. The pregnant blonde was radiant. So much so, she was practically bursting with happiness, and Gretchen was truly glad for her. If only she wasn't so dang lonely herself, she thought sadly, reaching into the off-white, antique fridge for a cold water.

"Oh yes, please," Elissa gasped, chugging from the proffered bottle greedily.

Gretchen sighed and shook her head, looking over the chairs and the small magazine table that had just been delivered. They were arranged in an *L* shape, nine in total, and were perfect for the waiting area at the front of the salon.

Colors were her jam, the brighter and happier the better. And not just as far as interior design went. Heck no! That included hair, nails, tattoos, and makeup too. So far, her salon had been repainted with new lighting installed, and she'd ordered the orange, well more like tangerine colored chairs almost immediately. The walls were a creamy white for the most part, to make the most of the space since mirrors abounded anyway. But all the accents were tangerine or pink, including the moldings.

*Cut It Out* was truly taking shape and Gretchen could scarcely believe it was hers. Back home in Iowa she'd been a chubby little nobody living with her elderly uncle and mean spirited cousins. The Kaepernick's weren't known for having much in the way of compassion, but they'd taken her in when her parents had died tragically in an automobile accident.

Iowa was as far away now as she wanted it to be. Her memories were nothing good. No, life had only truly started for her when she'd arrived in the garden State after being certified as a stylist. She'd found an apartment to rent with Elissa and had managed to save enough to complete her business degree through online courses.

She did not want to spend her life working for peanuts for other people. Whoever said hard work paid off was not lying, she thought and looked around at the space she was already starting to love.

*"It wooks gweat, Gwech,"* her bestie said with a mouthful of chocolate chunk cookie.

Gretchen understood and beamed at her bestie's praise. She sat down next to Lissa and hugged her around the shoulders, the two of them squealing like they did when they lived together and something good happened to either of them. She had to be careful though because of Elissa's condition.

Gretchen just could not believe it. Elissa was having a baby! Her rounded belly was peaking slightly over the tie-dyed waistband of her yoga pants, but Gretchen's BFF was rocking that bump. The smoldering looks Elissa got from her total hottie of a hubby the last few days she'd been around them were proof of that.

*Yowza!*

It was enough to make a girl blush. Well, a girl who hadn't seen anything resembling a penis in far too long. She was not promiscuous by any means, but Gretchen had always had a healthy appreciation for sex.

Not that she'd had any kind of sex in a long, *long, very long* time. Anyway, wasn't Hunter a doll to have his buddy Trigger drive Elissa over to see her? The cute guy had even offered to go out and grab them all some lunch.

"You sure trigger's got a girlfriend, Jessica?" Gretchen asked Elissa's sister-in-law who'd come by to help along with her pal, Kylie.

The big man in question had just gotten out of his truck and was heading for the door with a sack of sandwiches for the women.

"Yep. Going on five years," Elissa answered for her, and turned her head with a wide smile for the man himself. "Thanks, Trigger. I'm starved."

"Always a pleasure, Nari," he replied, using some strange nickname for Lissa that had her blushing before he headed back outside.

"You know, he doesn't have to wait out there,"

Gretchen began, but Lissa was already shaking her head.

"He's fine, really, he, *um*, has a podcast he listens to. It's all good. Here, want half of mine and I'll take half of yours?"

"Sure," Gretchen said, shaking her head.

*Same old Lissa. Sigh.*

She was getting pretty fed up with herself and that certain little green-eyed monster that kept popping up. She couldn't help it. She was not jealous in a bad way of her friend's happiness. She just wanted a little somethin' for herself. Was that too much to ask?

Elissa had hit the equivalent of the *romantic mega million* in lottery terminology. Gretchen was in awe. She still couldn't believe her former roomie was having a baby this soon after meeting, and *marrying* the insanely hot, sexy as sin, construction mogul that was Hunter Maverick.

"What?" Elissa asked.

"I was just wondering when you were gonna teach me your secrets to living a wildly passionate and successful lifestyle," she replied deadpan.

"Gretchen! *Stahp it,*" she replied, blushing furiously.

Her Hudson County accent always came out

more pronounced when she was excited or emotional, something Gretchen thought was ridiculously cute.

"No secrets, honest. Look, you are going to find someone who loves you for you, I just know it. Now, first things first, when will you be ready to take on clients? I seriously need a pedicure," Elissa said sticking her swollen feet out.

"*Dayum girl!* Put those crusty things away! I am trying to eat," Gretchen teased.

"Seriously, I got a *ick* thing about feet," Jessica seconded.

"You two are nuts," Kylie chimed in, grabbing her turkey sandwich with lettuce, tomato, and mayo from the sack.

Gretchen smiled at their playful shenanigans as she passed around sodas and waters to Elissa, Jessica, and Kylie. The four women had spent nearly all of that morning getting Gretchen's salon ready for her big opening day.

*Cut It Out* was her first solo business venture, and nerves abounded. She had been in the hair biz for over a decade, but that was not the same as running a salon.

True, Gretchen had worked for various bosses, doing hair and nails, and even provided in-home services for a while, but this was her ultimate *profes-sional* dream. She was finally going to be in charge of her own business.

Of course, Gretchen was still a bit nervous, but she was hoping with all her might that it would all work out. All her business classes really helped her create a marketing plan, and she was almost positive it was going to work. Maverick Point had been sans beauty salon for months now and *Cut It Out* was going to fill a void in the New Jersey town.

*It just has to be successful.*

She'd sunk every last dime she had into this venture. Including taking out a small loan to pay for a few new necessities, like the chairs, updated appliances, various hair care products, aprons, brooms, lights, marketing materials, a few small advertisements placed strategically on the internet, and in the local paper, and other odds and ends.

"Well, I can't wait to sit down in one of these for some highlights," Kylie said. "Maybe I'll get some like yours," the pixie-cut blonde mused, looking at the chunky purple and royal blue locks that Gretchen had added to her newly dark locks earlier that week.

"Maybe, but I think maybe you should be scheduling a pedi appointment too," she teased her new friend who wiggled her unpolished toes.

"What? They have character!"

"Yeah, right? And you teased me," Lissa said, stealing a chip from Jess.

"I can't help going barefoot, it feels too nice," Kylie explained.

The woman really did not like shoes. Gretchen shook her head and laughed. It was the first time she'd ever seen anyone move furniture without anything to cover what was probably the easiest to bruise part of any person. Her toes. But she had to admit, Kylie proved remarkably agile on her feet.

"Okay, for all of your efforts on my behalf, I announce you shall get your first pedicure on the house. And that goes for all of you ladies!"

All three women clapped, and Gretchen giggled, so happy she was liable to bust. She had two hair-stylists coming to work, and more lined up for inter-views the following week. She was going to need a lot of help. At least, she would soon once she built a steady clientele.

All that took was some time, some good quality output, and the trust of the community. *Cut It Out* was going to be amazing. She was going to show the Maverick Point community that this was *the* place for all their hair care and beauty needs.

"Don't you go getting worried on me now," Elissa

said. "I told you, Hunter is going to tell all of the Pri-, I mean, all of his *employees* about this place. You'll be fine, Gretch. Better than fine."

"I sure hope so," she said, biting her lip nervously.

Speak of the devil, Hunter just arrived with Brayden, Jessica's boyfriend. The women insisted their significant others join them for lunch.

"There is more than enough," Gretchen said handing out some of the extra subs Trigger had bought.

Seriously, he'd gotten like ten for the four of them. Gretchen was a big girl, but she couldn't put away more than one-foot-long sandwich on her best day. Even if the other women had managed to polish off two each.

"Thank you, Gretchen," Hunter replied, his eyes on his wife as he sat beside her.

Brayden had the same besotted look as he snuggled close to Jess feeding her bites of his sandwich, even though she'd eaten. Gretchen had never seen anything like it.

*There must be something in the Maverick Point water,* she mused. Or maybe it was the mountain air? Hell, they'd even cleaned up.

*What prizes,* she thought, and tried not to watch as each man held hands with their women and cuddled them close after cleaning the remnants of their mini feast. When Elissa began to yawn, Hunter moved.

"I'm fine," she argued.

"She's tired," Gretchen said right to Hunter who seemed to growl and nod.

"Better get you to bed," he told Elissa who's face had gone bright pink.

"Whoooo! It's getting' hot in here," Kylie replied loudly, and everyone laughed.

Except Hunter. His teal eyes seemed to glow as he gazed at the love of his life. There was no doubt about it. He was crazy about her, and she really deserved to have someone like that. Perfect husband that he was, he scooped her up and brought her to the car despite her protests.

Gretchen's heart squeezed as she watched them. It was a helluva thing being happy on one hand and desperately lonely on the other. *Maybe someday*, she thought, *just maybe.*

"I'll drop by tomorrow," Elissa shouted as Hunter buckled her in and nodded his goodbyes to Gretchen.

*Sigh. How romantic.*

# Chapter Two

Gretchen had always wanted something like that for herself. Not the feeding by hand or the carrying bit per se, but a man who would pamper and take care of her just like Elissa had with Hunter. *Some things just weren't meant to be,* she supposed and shrugged. She had too much to do to stand there moping.

She got back to work with a vengeance. After moving a few more boxes to the storage room at the back of the store, Gretchen, Kylie, Brayden, and Jessica placed some last finishing touches on the front of the place before the rest of the gang left.

She thanked them all profusely and gave them coupons for on the house treatments at their convenience, of course. Brayden blushed when she handed him one, but Jessica insisted he take it.

"Men don't get pedicures---"

"You would be surprised," Gretchen replied, shaking her head.

"Seriously, you need one," Jessica said, taking his hand as they left.

She laughed and waved them away. It was silly how many America men did not believe in frequenting salons. Younger crowds had more modern attitudes, and times were changing, but Gretchen had a feeling she would have an easier time pulling teeth than getting the men of Hunter's company, Maverick Development, to become regular clients.

No matter She would just have to prove her services too good to miss. Determination had her scrubbing floors, hefting garbage away to the dumpster in the back, and wiping mirrors for the third time that night before she was too exhausted to continue.

When she was as finished as she was ever going to be, Gretchen headed upstairs to her apartment which was located directly above the salon.

Thankfully, the space was much larger than she'd

thought when she'd first looked at the building from the outside. The location was prime, situated on one of Maverick Point's busiest streets.

In fact, the older woman, whose lease Gretchen was taking over, had converted the two top apartments into one, rather spacious, two-story, housing unit. Clean, polished wood floors were gleaming from the thorough washing and polishing Gretchen had given them after the movers had left.

She'd discarded most of her old, scratched furniture, keeping only the main pieces like her dresser, an old leather couch, a small dinette set, and a few bookshelves.

Before heading down to meet the girls, she'd left the windows open, and the essential oil diffuser on while she worked on the salon. Grateful now for her forethought, Gretchen breathed in the clean smells and smiled contentedly.

The whole place had a clean, fresh scent, and she hummed a tune happily as she walked around closing windows and locking them. For a minute there, she had thought she'd never get the smells of bleach, furniture polish, and window washer out of her nostrils, but thankfully, she was wrong about that.

"This is gonna work. Life's gonna be so good from now on," she told herself, giving herself a little pep talk.

Gretchen had spent most of her youth being ignored and trying to remain that way. Growing up chubby was not something her trim uncle and athletic cousins approved of. She'd been taunted and made fun of, especially when she showed an interest in hair.

*"Who in the world is gonna go to you to make themselves look good?"* Cousin Alfred had told her when she finally packed her bags after high school.

Well, Gretchen had been successfully employed as a stylist for a decade now, so the answer to his snotty question was plenty of folks! She was painfully shy when she was younger, but not anymore.

Having a fuller figure was not a negative, at least that was how Gretchen saw it. She loved her body, her extra curves and love handles, and her unique sense of style. She had a gift for beauty, and a knack for making others look their very best, and Gretchen was not afraid to use either.

She had spent most of her time much since arriving on the storefront, so upstairs, where she would live, was still a bit of a mess. Not dirty, but definitely unorganized. Half a dozen sturdy storage boxes sat piled in the hallway, waiting to be unpacked, but she was too worn out to get to it tonight.

At least the bedroom was all done, she thought, and walked past the new king-sized bed she'd bought herself. It was the one item she'd splurged on. A business necessity, she had convincingly told herself since she'd be on her feet twelve to fourteen hours a day, and therefore, needed to sleep well at night to feel ready and refreshed.

Giggling at the way she'd spun that tale, even if only to herself, Gretchen headed for the master bathroom. It was not overly large, but it was bigger than the one she'd previously had. Neat and clean after the good bleaching she'd given it, she took a moment to admire the gauzy curtain she'd hung up over the window next to an antique oval mirror in a painted frame.

Blue glass tiles lined the floors and the walls, offset by creamy white trim and a large pedestal sink. A bar for hand and bath towels was mounted to the wall, and there was a wire rack for toilet paper. She'd already added a shelf for her hair dryer, curling iron, and makeup, and there was a large linen cabinet against the wall that held towels and other toiletries, giving the whole room a friendly finished look.

The shower was her absolute favorite. Whoever had lived there before had removed the sheetrock wall that separated the bedroom from the shower, replacing that with eight inch glass bricks. The effect was scintillating. A sort of, naughty little peepshow of the person showering for anyone on the other side.

*Kinky*, she thought, as she settled under the warm spray of water.

Two could definitely fit inside the large stall. Smiling at the image of her and some hot fantasy guy, she gave herself over to the imagery and sighed under the warm spray of water. There was even a seat built into the wall that should certainly come in handy for some *smexy fun in the shower times.*

If only the occasion arose so Gretchen could test her theory. She picked up her loofah and body wash and built a good lather to wash away the aches and pains of the day's activities. Moving furniture was not exactly her calling.

Gretchen was used to being on her feet for long

hours, sometimes trekking her equipment to people's houses or hotels for work. She specialized in fancy updos and had catered to plenty a bridezilla in her time. But this was a different kind of sore. Her aches had aches, for pity's sake!

"Owie," she groaned, and stretched her muscles.

Stylists had to have good endurance, and she had that in spades. Muscles were a different thing all together. She has always been on the fluffier side of the totem pole. Who was she kidding? Gretchen was more than fluffy. She had big, heavy breasts. Triple D's that required serious support. Beneath those bad girls were belly rolls, large hips, plenty of ass, and some serious thunder thighs.

*Sigh.*

There was no sugarcoating it. And why should she even try? What you see was what you get with Gretchen. She was what her grandmother had called *pleasantly plump,* back before she'd been orphaned and sent to live with her uncle.

She was a good, solid size sixteen, with no apologies. Rolling her eyes in pleasure as she ran the loofah over her elbows, knees, and ankles, she washed away the grime and aches of the day's work.

Next, she grabbed a natural bath sponge and

squeezed more of the tiger blossom scented body wash onto it before working the soap into a lather over every single inch of her soft, curvy body. It was her favorite scent and would leave her skin feeling refreshed and silky smooth.

It had taken some doing, but she'd learned to love herself, rolls and all. She couldn't help her size. Had tried dieting and exercise, but after spending all day standing up doing people's hair, the last thing she wanted was to go to the gym.

She just liked food. Was that crime? And no, it wasn't all junk food, though she wouldn't mind another one of those decadent honey cream claws from the famous *Bear Claw Bakery* that was located right in the next town.

*Serious yum.*

Jessica had brought over half a dozen for her and the girls, but Elissa snuck the last two while the rest of them were polishing the bathroom fixtures. Darn her pregnancy-induced gluttony!

*Oh well.*

She'd probably needed it more than Gretchen did. Other than the occasional indulgence in sugary coated goodness, Gretchen stuck to grilled meats and fresh veggies for no other reason than because she liked them.

*So there.*

She wanted to stick her tongue out at all the judgmental people who assumed because she had some extra pounds, she must spend her time eating fast food and candy. The truth was, that sandwich Trigger had brought had been the first thing she'd eaten that she hadn't cooked in a long while.

She simply didn't have the extra cash to eat out. Even cheap take out. Not that she had to explain herself to anyone. Gretchen gave up on that a long time ago.

She sighed and stretched some more, allowing the flowery scent of her bath wash and the warm water to relax her. Thank goodness for good water pressure.

Gretchen lathered her hair with shampoo then conditioner, the good stuff so there were few bubbles but extra moisture and damage control she needed since she dyed it so often. She wondered what had possessed her to grow it.

She used to keep it super short because it was so thick, and it grew ridiculously fast. But ever since she'd started toying with the idea of landing a man of her own, she'd decided to grow out her hair.

How many times had she heard plenty a customer remark on how their boyfriends loved their hair long? So, while she did not have a boyfriend yet, she figured she might as well try it.

It was shoulder length now, healthy, and glossy and surprisingly easy to manage. She loved the different braids and twists she could put in it, not to mention the colors.

She might have started out growing it with a man in mind, but the truth was she liked it this length. It was a little bit extra, but Gretchen was a business owner now. Having good hair was kind of her whole shtick.

She dressed for bed, lying on the soft and fluffy duvet that smelled good and clean like her favorite fabric softener. Biting her lip, she felt her anxiety and excitement warring within her. Her new life was about to start, and she could not wait.

Maybe she should check her emails one last time before she went to sleep? Grabbing her cell phone, she opened the app and scrolled, hoping to see a reply to the missive she'd sent out recently.

*Sigh.*

Still no message from that famous matchmaker Elissa had told her about. Gretchen refused to let that worry her. Tomorrow was her big day. Finally, she was the proud owner of her own business, and her own boss.

If only she had someone to share it with, she thought and rolled onto her side, tucking the blanket under her chin. Uncle Uzzi probably had more important people to match up than a little nobody from Iowa like her.

But still, a girl could hope.

# Chapter Three

"Uncle Uzzi! I am so glad you dropped by," Elissa squeaked as her favorite person in the whole world, aside from her husband came strolling in.

Uncle Uzzi, matchmaker extraordinaire, walked across the threshold and opened his arms out to the pregnant Tiger Shifter. Elissa was so happy she returned the warm embrace as she would her own father's if he were still alive. Uncle Uzzi was a perfect surrogate.

"Look at you, darling. You are glowing," he said, and her smile grew even brighter.

There was something so warm and open about the amazing Witch that left the Nari feeling both relaxed and energized the second she was with him.

Maybe that was part of his magic, she mused, as he gazed at her with sparkling blue eyes.

"How is that mate of yours? Treating you well, yes?" he asked, with his trademark white hair and beard resting in place as if he'd just trimmed it.

The older man sat down at the table with Elissa right beside him. She noticed him looking around and laughed as she pulled out a dish of fresh-baked cookies, she'd been hiding on the chair next to her. He had a sweet tooth no one could deny.

"Ah! You were tricking an old man, shame on you," he teased.

"Was not! You're just in time," Elissa said, and pointed to a warm pot of herbal tea she'd just steeped. Paired with the cookies, the two of them were in for quite the treat.

"I was just about to have a snack. Won't you join me?" the Nari asked and giggled a little.

"Of course, and you need it, after all you're eating for two, or maybe three," Uncle Uzzi smirked.

"Oh my, I hadn't considered that," Elissa replied and swallowed hard.

"Yes, well, it is always a possibility with Shifters my dear," Uncle Uzzi said. "I was on my way out of town for an important emergency job, but I decided to swing over here to check on some things first."

"Really? Well, I'm glad you did."

"Yes. Also, I wanted to tell you in person that I got an email from your old roommate."

"Oh, you mean Gretchen? Yes, I told her about you, is that okay? I mean I should have probably asked---"

"Nonsense! Of course it is alright. But I wanted to ask you first, does Gretchen know anything about us?"

"What do you mean?"

"Does she know about magic, the paranormal world, Shifters in particular, dear Elissa?"

"Oh," Elissa murmured and flushed guiltily. "Not exactly, but neither did I when I met you, Uncle Uzzi."

"True, but you were a special case. Hmm, I may have to rethink my original plans then."

"So, you can't help her?" Elissa asked, sadness filling her eyes with tears.

She'd been so happy ever since she'd run into him that rainy night down the shore. Ever since he'd brought her to the Pride House where she first met and fell in love with Hunter. Elissa did not expect everyone to have the same luck she had been blessed with, but she really hoped Uncle Uzzi could help her friend.

"Now, now, I didn't say that," he hinted. "How about we catch up a bit first? Yes?" he asked and the two of them sat back and nibbled on their cookies, sipping tea, while they chatted.

Elissa absolutely adored Uncle Uzzi and loved his surprise visits. Especially since it usually meant someone was about to be mated. The Pride could use more mated pairs, she thought as she rubbed a hand over her belly.

The sound of someone approaching brought her head up. Uncle Uzzi's electric blue eyes sparkled, and Elissa swore she felt something electrify the air as they turned and watched one of Elissa's own security team enter the kitchen.

It was Reginald Cray. As usual, he was sporting a pair of disreputable jeans, even worse sneakers, and a tight black t-shirt with two holes in the hem. The clothes were worn, but they weren't that bad. Neither was the man inside of them for that matter.

*If only he believed that too*, she thought.

Like most Shifters, Reg had rippling muscles corded around his six-and-a-half-foot frame and his looks were beyond the average normal. He had a good face with a straight nose, stubborn chin, and midnight blue eyes.

Not many people noted the unique dark blue of

his gaze or the adorable way his bottom lip jutted out, slightly larger than the top lip. They couldn't get past the wildly uneven chop job of his thick brown hair and matching beard.

An idea began to take shape, Uncle Uzzi met her gaze, his own eyes twinkling with merriment. The notion now fully formed hopped around the Nari's head, desperate to get out, as she looked him over.

"*Oh my gah!*" Elissa spit out the bite of cookie she'd been nibbling.

The Tiger Shifter was one of the Nari's most trusted and elite guards, despite the rumors about his worth. Hunter trusted him, and so did she, and that was good enough for her.

She knew several members of the Pride still doubted his loyalties, but she did not share those concerns. Maybe it was time Reg found a little happiness. After all that business with Blake and that rogue streak that came through town a few months ago, he deserved it.

Elissa had sort of taken the Tiger under her wing. She'd asked her husband specifically for Reg to be her guard. Yes, he had unknowingly let the traitor who had tried to kill both her and her mate loose, but he honestly had no idea what the man was going to do.

Reg had known Blake for years, had worked under him and lived with him. That sort of bond did not just go away. Besides, he'd been young and impressionable, and that smooth talking ex-Beta had been a trusted friend once upon a time.

Blake had hidden his evil side for so long, and Reg was simply too trusting. Blake had first come to the Maverick Pride under the Neta's own recommendation. What else did a man need to gain the support of a young Shifter?

Reg had no experience with that kind of subterfuge. He'd been unaware of the ex-Beta's motives and thought he was simply doing his old friend a solid by releasing him. But like all of them, he had been betrayed by Blake. After the attack on Elissa, Hunter, the Neta of the Pride, had killed him in battle.

When it came time to decide Reg's punishment, Elissa had surprised everyone by speaking up for him. She'd forgiven him and voted he be placed as one of her own guards. Reg was a solid member of the Pride, and ever since then, he had worked desperately to make it up to both the Nari and the Neta.

"What is it? Is something wrong," Reg said, dropping into a fighting stance and looking around the otherwise empty room.

"When was the last time you cut your hair?" Elissa wondered aloud.

"Uh, what, Nari?" the man dropped his hands and cocked his head.

"Yes, I was wondering that myself," Uncle Uzzi piped in.

"I am sorry, I don't understand what my hair has to do with---"

"I mean really, I know you guys are a bunch of pussies when it comes to water, but is it the same with scissors and razors?" Uncle Uzzi asked, eyebrows raised as if in shock.

"I'm not a pussy. I mean, I'm not afraid of water or anyt--- wait, what are you two talking about?"

"What I mean is no guard of the Nari's should walk around looking like that," Uncle Uzzi waved his hand at him, sparks of magic shooting from the tips.

"Ow!" reg squeaked when one landed on his face. The young Tiger smacked himself, putting out the fire the old Witch's magic had accidentally started on his facial hair.

"Oops. Sorry, that happens occasionally," the Witch replied, and smiled a little.

"It's fine," growled Reg, staring back at them with part of his beard missing.

"Oh, come on, it's not that bad," Elissa tried.

She failed miserably when it came to finding a reasonable defense for the Witch's magic zapping him. Shrugging it off, she focused on her obviously uncomfortable guard.

"You need a haircut, period," she stated.

"What's going on in here?" Hunter Maverick sauntered into the room, making a beeline for his wife and the cub she was carrying.

He dropped a quick, deep kiss on her mouth and cradled her face in his hands before greeting Uncle Uzzi with a handshake and pat on the back. Finally, he turned and looked at his Pride mate.

"Damn, Reg," he looked the man up and down. "You look like hell."

"Yeah, well, my beard was just set on fire," he muttered.

"What? No, I mean the whole look. What happened, we run out of razors?" Hunter asked.

"Look, I tried to go by Lou's Barbershop the other day, but he's out of town."

"If you want, I can do you like me," Hunter grinned, and rubbed his smooth head.

The Neta of the Maverick Pride had plenty of

hair, but he preferred to shave his dome. To be honest, Elissa loved the sexy bald look on her hot as hell mate.

She pressed closer to him, and without hesitation, his strong arms wrapped around her, enveloping her in his love. She was a lucky woman to have found her fated mate, and she owed her thanks to Uncle Uzzi. Stealing a glance at the white-haired Witch, Elissa watched as his blue gaze seemed glued to Reg.

*Hmm.*

"No way- uh, I mean, no, *thank you*, Neta," Reg replied, averting his gaze, and baring his throat as a sign of respect to the leader of the Pride.

One more point in his loyalty basket, Elissa thought, thoroughly approving of him. Only the most self-assured and loyal Tigers could so willingly submit to another Shifter regarding of his or her dominance.

These manners or acts of respect were not weakness. In fact, quite the opposite. And Reg, of all the Tiger Guard in the Maverick Pride was the first who came to mind when she thought of quiet strength and unwavering loyalty.

"You know," Uncle Uzzi began, and Elissa could not stop a smile from breaking out across her face.

*He was gonna do it, wasn't he? Eeeeek! How exciting!*

"The Nari's best friend just opened a salon in town. Isn't that right, Elissa?"

"Why, yes, Uncle Uzzi, that is correct," she replied, already knowing where this was headed.

Hells to the yeah. Elissa was completely on board.

"Uh, isn't that for women?" Reg asked.

"Nonsense. It's a unisex salon. Besides, your Nari would want the Pride to make her friend feel welcomed, wouldn't she?" Uncle Uzzi pressed.

Reg's dark blue eyes glittered for a moment. He was far from stupid and could probably smell their set up. But too bad. Elissa was moody and pregnant, and she was in charge, dammit.

"Uncle Uzzi, you are a genius! I should have thought of this already. Reg, I would like you to go get a haircut."

"What? I mean, why?"

"Well, you're my best guard, and I can't have you looking like that," she gestured, and almost felt bad when the man blushed.

"Sh--- I mean, sorry. Yes, Nari," he said, "but who will go with you to the market? It's on your schedule---"

"I think I can handle anything my mate wants to do today, Reg. You go on."

"Yes, Reg, go on. A haircut is exactly what you need."

"Okay," he answered.

Elissa exchanged a secret look with Uncle Uzzi and crossed her fingers. With any luck, Uncle Uzzi had found Gretchen the perfect man, *er*, mate.

*Squeee!*

She sure hoped her bestie was as openminded as she was about the whole turning into something *furry* and *purry* thing these Maverick Pride fellas did.

Biting her lip, Elissa wondered if there was some way she could have maybe prepared her bestie for this first. Oh well. It was too late now. She said a silent prayer for both her friend and her Pride mate.

"Reginald?" Uncle Uzzi stopped him.

"Yes, Uncle Uzzi?"

"Be sure to tell Gretchen that I said hello," Uncle Uzzi said with a twinkle in his eye, and a smile on his face.

*Oh yes,* Elissa sighed. She was so full of love and happiness. Content, safe, and sound in her mate's strong arms, she leaned back, letting him bear her weight.

The Nari had a feeling that everything was going to be *purrfectly* fine.

*Prrrrrrr.*

# Chapter Four

Of all the ridiculous shit he'd ever heard.

*Get a haircut, Reg.*

Like, seriously? What the actual fuck? It wasn't like Reg worked as a fashion model. Was it his fault his hair grew like nobody's business? Or that the only barber in town left unexpectedly?

He wasn't some dandy-Lion Shifter going to pieces over his hair, like those ridiculous males did all the freaking time. Lion males were such babies about their manes.

Not Reg. He was a Tiger Shifter and held a coveted position in the Nari's private guard. He didn't have time for this crap. And yet, there he was. Outside of some loud orange and pink salon called *Cut It Out.*

*At least the name was cute*, he thought. Reg growled, annoyed that he was even there. He hopped out of his blood red Jeep Wrangler XE Rubicon, with special modifications he'd ordered that were put in at a specialty Shifter-run auto shop.

Those additions were typically necessary for Shifters. His Jeep needed to carry not just a man of his height and bulk, but several at a time while also maintaining a modicum of comfort should he have the Nari, or other females in his presence. The bullet proof body and glass were just bonuses.

Reg loved that vehicle. It was his first major adult purchase. He especially loved it when he could take the top off and let the wind fly all around him.

Spring was crisp and cold in this part of the Garden State, but nothing his thick hide couldn't handle. It was the rain that kept him from taking the top off just then.

Maverick Point tended to get a little wet weather every day around this time of year, and soggy seats were no fun for anyone. Maybe he'd take the top off on the upcoming weekend if it was sunny enough.

Fuck. He could not believe he had to have some human female friend of his Nari cut his hair. Shrugging off his misgivings, Reg stomped down the sidewalk to where the new salon was located. Well, technically, it was in the same spot as the old salon, but he'd never stepped foot in Mrs. Bower's place before.

Thank fuck his brother, Rob, was overseas and couldn't see him now. His big bro was a Navy Seal and spent most of his time away from Maverick Point. Occasionally, he'd email Reg or send him some wild or exotic thing he'd found when he wasn't out on some mission or other.

*Damn.*

Reg missed his big bro. He wouldn't have gotten mixed up in Blake's shitstorm if Robbie was home. But that was no one's fault but his own, and he knew it. He only meant Rob would have seen through that faithless prick. Reg had been trying to make up for his mistake ever since. Thank the gods for the Nari. Her quiet belief in him had been the only thing that had kept Reg going for a while there.

Yes, he'd royally fucked up by even doubting his Neta when Blake had been whispering poison in his ear. That Shifter had been pure evil.

Reg was ashamed by how easily he'd been manipulated by that dickless motherfucker. Blake had told Reg that he had to help him protect the Neta, even if from himself.

He claimed Elissa was going to harm Hunter's

rule, that a human female would be his downfall. Blake claimed Shifters *had to* mate other Shifters. He did not believe she was strong enough to take a seat beside Hunter, and that she would out them all.

The Shifter secret was one they could not survive without keeping. Everyone knew that. But Blake hadn't counted on the *Puspa,* which had changed Elissa from a normal human woman to a rare and powerful White Tiger Shifter.

Unfortunately, Reg had trusted Blake, giving him what he needed to escape. He didn't know the man had become unstable and his views fanatical. That whole keeping the blood pure was ridiculous in Reg's opinion.

He'd expected Blake to flee, not try to kill the Nari. He would never have aided him in doing that. It had taken too long for Reg to see that all Blake's supposed good intentions were really just a completely psychotic jealousy that had eaten away his reason. Reg's mistake had almost cost the lives of his Neta and Nari.

The Alpha couple had been in harm's way because of him, and he'd never felt worse about anything in his life.

Luckily, his Neta was strong. He'd put an end to the threat himself, and Reg had been in awe of the man ever since. Hunter Maverick was a fierce leader and a good man.

His mate had not sapped his strength like Blake had said she would. In fact, Elissa only made him stronger, *better,* and most wondrous of all, she had made the man happy. *Truly happy.*

Hell, Reg had never seen the Neta smile so much. If that's what a human mate did for a Shifter, well then, they could sign Reg up. He was completely ready to meet his one and only be she human, Shifter, Witch, or whatever.

He was ready for a sweet female of his own.

*Grrr,* his inner beast grumbled approvingly, and Reg knew the beast was feeling the need for a mate as much as his human side.

Maybe he'd have a chat with Uncle Uzzi if the old Witch was still at the house when he returned. After this disaster. What kind of haircut would he even get?

Reg pondered that while he walked past *Jessica's Closet.* Looking inside the newly replaced glass window, he shook his head remembering what went down.

A streak of rogue Tiger Shifters influenced by that unhappy fucker Blake had decided to come to Maverick Point to try to wreak havoc on the Pride.

Those assholes hadn't counted on the amazing females the Maverick Pride was blessed with. Ferocious and deadly, the she-Cats had beaten the fuck out of that scum, but Brayden had nearly ripped the one who'd threatened his mate in two.

Lost in the memory, Reg's eyes were unseeing until they met the unique teal stare of a certain tall redhead who happened to be the Neta's sister. Jessica Maverick waved, and Reg returned the gesture, smiling his hello.

Of course, he was also quick to acknowledge her big as fuck mate who happened to be standing beside the lovely she-Cat. Brayden bared his teeth and nodded, causing Reg to smirk.

The Beta was a bit growly and possessive when it came to his woman. Not that Reg blamed him. Shifters and possessiveness went hand in hand, or was that claw in claw, he wondered.

Either way. They were another happy pair. He nodded wistfully.

There was a time he'd found the Neta's sister a little more than cute, but the Fates had other ideas for Jessica Maverick. She'd found her mate in the new Pride Beta, Brayden Smith.

The Black Bear was formerly of the Barvale Clan, which was located one town over, but a series of events had led him to the Tiger Pride, and he'd never looked back.

Reg was glad for that. The man made one hell of an addition to the Pride. Even if he wasn't a sleek, gorgeous Tiger like some people. Reg grinned.

His animal's thoughts and feelings had a way of being a little bit outspoken at times. It was another reason he didn't resist the suggestion to go and get his hair cut. Whenever he neglected his grooming, his Tiger's fur tended to mimic his human self.

Unkempt locks were not a great look on him as a man, and as a beast they were downright ridiculous. His Tiger's fur tended to get long and scruffy, hardly presentable for the Nari's guard.

Even worse, he looked a bit like a young Lion cub than the awesome striped beast that he was. That was *unfuckingacceptable*.

He rubbed his hands over his face and paused. Fucking hell. He forgot all about the patch on his beard where Uncle Uzzi had set the hair on fire. Reg wondered if that was why Jessica had giggled when she saw him.

*Whatever.*

*Growl.*

*Easy buddy,* he told his beast.

He stopped and read the sign over the door, smirking before heading inside.

*Cut It Out.*

Great name. He especially liked the bold orange on black letters even if they were outlined in pink. His Tiger did too, approving the color scheme as if he had had any say in it.

The front of the salon had six stations with regular looking barber chairs, only these were covered in deep orange vinyl. The back of the long room held a few manicurist tables and four pedicure chairs along the wall.

The inside smelled new and fresh. Everything was crisp and clean and done in black, orange, and white. Again his Tiger chuffed happily. Maybe having his hair cut by a woman wouldn't be so bad.

He walked over to the reception desk and rang the little bell. Breathing deeply he was caught unawares as the scent of flowers filled his nostrils. Reg's Tiger seemed to go completely still at the strangely familiar and tantalizing fragrance.

*Easy,* Reg rolled his shoulders attempting to play off the fact that his heart was pounding and his pulse racing.

There was also some action going on right below his belt. What the fuck? His cock was rocking a semi, and he had to adjust himself, pulling his holey t-shirt out of his waistband so as to cover the bastard up.

Reg checked his phone. It was 9:45. The sign on the door said open at 10. So, he was a little early. Still, where was everyone?

"Hello?" he called out.

Following his nose, he tracked the delicious fragrance to the back of the salon. The scent grew stronger as he neared a door with a sign that read "storage" on the outside. Using his supernatural hearing abilities, Reg stilled as the person inside grunted and grumbled.

*"Frigging box. Had to put it on the top shelf. Short girl problems,"* the voice muttered.

It wasn't the words that had him stopped in his tracks, but the feeling of awareness that roared through his veins as the woman, *yes woman*, talked to herself.

Hand on the doorknob, Reg yanked it open, startling the creature inside into screaming, and nearly toppling off the small ladder she'd been standing precariously on.

*Oops.*

Lucky for her, Reg was a Tiger with faster than human reflexes and strength.

"Whoa!" she yelled.

"Gotcha," Reg replied, and thanked heaven for his speed as he scooped the lush female into his embrace with one arm, while catching the box she'd been wrestling with in the other.

"Wow, uh, thanks," the stranger whispered, her baby blue eyes sparkling up at him with surprise shining brightly in them.

*Holy hot mama.*

Whoever this delectable little female was, it was like she was calling out to his very soul with those beautiful eyes of hers. That sexy scent, and her sinfully gorgeous body were just bonuses.

"Beautiful," he whispered.

"Excuse me?" she replied, her voice a husky little sound that lit fires along his skin.

She licked her bottom lip and swallowed nervously, but all he could do was stare. Did she have any idea how scrumptious she was, clinging to his neck like that?

She had glossy brown hair pulled up in a loose, flattering ponytail with streaks of blue and purple showing in the back. Bright blue eyes, like robin's eggs, sparkled up at him, and her pale pink lips were moist and plump. She had skin like smooth cream with a pale smattering of freckles over the bridge of her small nose.

Reg wanted to lean in and catch those lips with his, see if they tasted as good as she smelled. Warm and fresh, like new spring flowers kissed by the sun. Exactly the kind his Tiger loved to roll around in on the base of Mount Maverick.

In fact, the beast seemed to like the idea of rolling around in her. She was the culmination of all his horny teenaged fantasies, but better. That fucking scent was making him braindead. His beast was riding him hard to take her, right then and there. Press her against the wall, tear the clothes from her flesh, and fuck her until neither one of them recalled their names.

*Shit.*

# Chapter Five

That reminded him, he didn't know her name. Warning bells started going off, this was the Nari's friend, but even that thought did not stop his cock from growing harder. Hell, the second he'd touched her, he was a goner.

Reg's Tiger pressed under his skin, growling and scratching, agitated beyond reason. Awareness made his breathing come hard and fast, and desire coursed through his body. He scented her reciprocal arousal and Reg's blood roared in his ears.

*Mate.*

Oh fuck.

*Mine.*

Slow down.

*No.*

She was it. She was the one. *His one*. Reg's true and fated mate.

*Holy fucking shit.*

"Uh, hi, I'm Gretchen. You can, um, put me down now," the woman said.

She smiled tightly, and raised her eyebrows expectantly, but there was no fucking way he was letting her go.

*Mine*, growled his beast, but Reg remained silent.

"Um, yeah. Okay, buddy. Thanks for the rescue, but it can't be easy holding me like this, so, you can just put me down, yeah? Like now."

Eyes narrowed, the tiny female pushed against his chest as if she could possibly move him. He was grinning like an idiot, but he couldn't help it. He was so damned happy.

*A mate! Whooopeeee!*

"Dude, what the heck?"

*Shit.*

He realized belatedly that she was trying to get away. Reg loosened his hold as sanity slowly came back to him. What the fucking fuck had just happened?

"Are you hard of hearing? Put me down."

"Sorry." He cleared his throat to try to get the

Tiger out of his voice, while letting her slide to the ground.

"I didn't expect to meet you. I guess, I'm shocked is all."

"What are you talking about? Who else did you expect to meet in my salon? Who are you?" Gretchen asked.

"Well, I mean, I came to get a haircut---"

"Okay, great," she said, pushing herself out of his arms.

Reg frowned. He missed the feel of her already and was about to step closer when he saw her expression. Shit. She was not loving this.

Okay, he could back off. For now. But fuck, she was warm and soft, like a living dream. One he could hold close and keep safe forever in his embrace.

*Fuck*, he sounded like an idiot even to himself.

She was talking again, and he tried to focus on her instead of his own insecurities, and his randy Tiger urging him to claim her right there.

"Congratulations! You're my very first walk-in client here at *Cut It Out*," she announced proudly.

"Excellent," he grinned, following as she proceeded to walk in front of him with the cutest little sway to her hips he'd ever seen.

His Tiger peeked out from his gaze, and it was all

he could do to wrestle the beast back down. Reg was simply struck by this woman on a level he'd never experienced. Could it be the universe had answered his most fervent wish? Had his mate finally been revealed?

Anticipation was climbing as he waited to see just what the sexy little female would say or do next. He already knew he would do anything for her. She was astounding, exceptional, purrfect for him in every way.

His gaze roamed over her ample curves, and he drooled. *Fucking drooled* just thinking of how good it was going to feel sliding along her soft creamy skin. Reg was a big Tiger, a big man, and he paused for a second to ponder whether she could take him.

*Fuck yeah, she could.*

The Fates would not have set them up otherwise. It would be tight though, and hot, so fucking hot. His dick hardened uncomfortably in his jeans, and he had to bite his tongue to stop the growl spilling from his lips. If little Miss Hotness didn't stop that sexy little switch in her walk, they were both going to find out just how well they fit together.

*Grrrrrr.*

It wasn't just her amazing heart-shaped ass that had him staring like a love-struck teen. It was the whole package. From this vantage point, he could take it all in with his unblinking predator's gaze.

*Shoulders, hips, heels.*

Even the way she landed on her feet with each step was adorable. It added a subtle bounce to her perfect ass he found irresistible. Reg wanted to ask her a million questions. They rushed forward, on the tip of his tongue, but he needed to tread carefully.

He did not want to rush her. Not at all. For now, he would simply enjoy the view. Her gaze seemed to take in every angle of the store as they left the closet and headed to the main area.

It was nice, as far as he could tell, but what did he know about salons? He'd never even been in one. Reg liked the colors and the fact it was clean and aesthetically pleasing. But what he really enjoyed was her pride and confidence as she led the way to a salon chair.

Gretchen smirked as she opened a new smock and shook it out while he sat down in the seat. That sassy little grin and her spunky attitude making her even more appealing.

*Simply gorgeous,* he thought with a purr stuck somewhere deep in his throat.

"Here we go," she said, draping the cloth over his body, and fuck, did he love her nearness.

She swallowed, not loudly, but he was a Tiger with supernaturally enhanced hearing. The sweet scent of flowers tickled his nose and Reg barely restrained himself from stealing a kiss.

She would not have welcomed it just then. He could tell that much about her already. Would she slap him? He wondered, weighing the pros and cons. A kiss would be worth the slap, but he didn't want to frighten her or turn her off by moving too quickly.

The female called to his Tiger in a way no other woman ever had. He needed her like he needed to take his next breath. There wasn't a thing about the woman he wasn't attracted to.

She wore ballerina flats on her tiny little feet, and if he wasn't mistaken, she had some kind of flower tattooed there. It was only just visible on the side of her left foot.

A fan of ink himself, he wondered what other secrets she had hidden beneath her clothes. Reg licked his lips as his eyes kept going back to her thick, long legs and luscious backside as she walked around the chair getting this and that and whatever she needed to do the job.

Her body was gorgeous, even though she'd probably dressed for comfort versus style. Lord knows he'd never found a woman's outfit particularly appealing, but this woman. Hell, he liked everything about her.

The tight black jeans paired with a soft gray shirt hugged her delectable curves, showcasing her sweet breasts and hips and he could just imagine her thighs parting and cradling his big body. He was a big man, Shifters generally were, and he always preferred his woman thick and soft.

She looked amazing. Totally fucking gorgeous, he thought.

*Mine,* his Tiger growled again. This time with a side of panting.

"I can shampoo you and get you prepped, my other stylist should be here any minute," she repeated, blinking at him slowly.

Reg was still holding the box he'd taken from her in the closet, and she seemed to only just notice, blushing as she took it from his lap and dropped it on the table behind the reception desk.

*Stylist?*

What fucking stylist? He wanted her.

*Shit.*

He was messing this up. Reg started, confused as to why she didn't recognize him as her mate, surely, she should have by now. Then realization dawned as she continued talking.

This was his Nari's best friend, and she was anormal. A normal who did not know a thing about Shifters or mates or Fate.

*Shit.*

"Stylist?" he said, clearing his throat.

"Yes, I have two new employees coming in today. Well, everyone is new, since we are new," she replied and giggled, a delightful sound to his ears.

The chair was right beside the reception desk, and he watched her lean over to grab an appointment calendar from the tidy desk.

"Bonnie and Marion are my first employees. I just need your name for the book," she said, checking the date and time.

But Reg didn't need to know her employees' names. He already knew who he wanted cutting his hair.

"My name is Reg Cray, and there's no need to wait for them, Gretchen."

"Oh, but they'll only be a few minutes," she started.

Reg shook his head, thinking how cute she looked with her brows drawing together as she looked from the calendar then back to him.

"I want you," he said simply.

*Mine.*

# Chapter Six

Gretchen's heart nearly stopped when the stranger, a big, sexy, hunk of man if she'd ever seen one, walked into her storeroom closet and startled her into falling off the ladder she'd been using to reach a box of hair products.

Someone had put the dang thing on the highest shelf, which for her, was impossible to get to without a ladder, and even then, it proved difficult.

Of course, *Mr. Tall Dark and Scruffy As Fuck* made up for it by catching her, *fluffy ass and all*, and with one hand no less!

*Holy cow*, she thought as she gave him the once over.

Despite his unruly locks and patchy beard- was

that a burn? The stranger was drop-dead gorgeous. Like most of the men in this town seemed to be for some reason.

*Must be the water*, she thought. Even the women of Maverick Point, which sat at the base of a mountain of the same name, seemed to be ridiculously good looking. Like way better than average.

Elissa's sister-in-law, Jessica, was just about the prettiest thing Gretchen had ever seen. Tall and curvy, she had the most amazing head of red hair. Being something of a hair afficionado, Gretchen was itching to get her hands on it.

Even her new friend, Kylie, was cute as a button with short blonde curls that curved towards her pretty pixie face. Kylie lived in the apartment above *Jessica's closet*, the boutique right next door. She designed and made the most amazing lingerie that Gretchen had ever seen for women of all shapes and sizes.

That was something Gretchen greatly appreciated. *Kisses By Kylie* featured designs that were not only sexy, but also extremely comfortable for women with bigger assets. Her pretty green eyes had sparkled with mischief when she'd showed Gretchen some of her naughtier confections.

Then there was Elissa. Her bestie had always

been a beauty, but even more so now with her pregnancy glow and the knowledge that she was loved.

Elissa deserved happiness. She was so sweet and caring, but that wasn't anything new to Gretchen. She'd lived with the woman and had been friends with her for years.

As a welcome present, Kylie had gifted Gretchen with the prettiest navy blue panty and bra set she had ever seen. She just couldn't wait to wear it. They never had demi-cup bras in her size, and she'd been dying for one.

The navy silk was so fine it was almost sheer, but the way it was sewn together offered her ample bosoms much needed support while maintaining the sexy feel of the set. The panties were cut high on the thigh and covered her belly while offering a seamless Brazilian cut bottom with no-show lines.

She couldn't wait to wear them. It was a shame she didn't have someone special in her life to warrant such a fancy set. She'd tucked both bra and panty away in her drawer, wrapped in tissue paper, just waiting for a special occasion.

Not that she needed a man to wear sexy lingerie, but it would be nice. Oh well. She was resigned to the fact she would likely be wearing them for herself on some girls' night out or a

Netflix binge night. She was used to being cast as the chubby friend in the movie that was her life.

*Always a bridesmaid,* she sighed heavily at the thought.

Gretchen was a big girl, but she loved herself and was comfortable in her skin just the same. Even if she was heavier than most.

The stranger who'd startled her and caught her with amazing strength and speed had stunned her into silence. Being in the sexy man's arms, even briefly, had all her secret places in a tingle.

*What the heck?*

She blinked rapidly, knowing she should just quit while she was ahead. But it felt so good, so right. Like she was supposed to be in his arms, if that made any sense.

But it didn't. She had to work to snap herself out of her momentary daydream about him slamming her up against the wall and kissing the daylights out of her.

*Yowza.*

The image was promising.

*What? No. Bad girl!*

Gretchen was running a business, not a lonely hearts club for fluffy chicks, for fuck's sake. Finally, after she'd gotten him to release her, she walked with him to the front of the store.

She knew she would feel better if she could just keep this professional and squash the alarmingly quick attraction she'd felt for the stranger. Gretchen was a realist. She was not stunning like Jessica, cute like Kylie, or lovely like Elissa.

She was just Gretchen Kaepernick. A boring brunette with a boring name. Well, not boring exactly. She'd added a few bright blue and purple highlights to the sides and bottom of her thick hair. The colorful streaks were especially visible when she wore it up. Like she was now.

Her tattoos were her best asset as far as she was concerned. Gretchen loved body art and from what she could see peeking out under the sleeve of his t-shirt, the handsome stranger had some of his own. Looked like something on the back of his arms and she wondered if it was a whole piece and how far it went across his enormous body.

*Do not think about his body,* she ordered herself.

Tapping her neatly trimmed nails with their fresh coat of polish on the counter, she tried not to think about how good it would feel to trace the lines of his tribal ink on those bulging biceps of his.

No piercings that she could see, though she

wouldn't mind either way. Gretchen limited her own to her ears, but she was still a fan. She had nine tattoos. Most were in places easily covered, but just lately she'd toyed with the idea of adding another on her shoulder. More likely she'd just start coloring in her largest piece.

She'd never shown it to anyone, except Elissa. Being single for over a year now, there was just no occasion to show it off. The tattoo wrapped around her right hip, touching the top of her right buttock, and reaching up to the underside of her breast. It had taken over six months to finish, but it was worth it.

The image depicted a tiger blossom tree, her favorite scent, and a big, beautiful Bengal tiger stretched out underneath the foliage. When she'd come across the images separately in a tattoo parlor, she'd begged the artist to combine them in a way she'd never seen before, and the result was stunning. Gretchen loved it.

Though the piece was mainly black, she'd had the woman add just a hint of orange and pink to the blossoms. For some reason, she'd also had the tiger's eyes colored in a deep, dark blue. The artist had laughed and said tiger's eyes were yellow, but Gretchen wanted them blue.

She'd always been fascinated by the big, striped cats. They were by far her favorite animal. So regal and majestic. The stranger, what did he say his name was? Oh yeah, Reg. Well, he sort of reminded her of a tiger.

It was in the way he carried himself, like he was stalking her instead of walking behind her. She wondered if he was a tiger in the bedroom.

Blushing at her thoughts, she turned and smiled at him, trying to distance herself behind her new businesswoman persona.

*"I want you,"* he'd said with a deep rumble in his voice that made her knees weak and panties wet.

*Gulp.*

"Thank you, um, but I would prefer to give my stylists the first clients. You know, to build confidence in the shop."

"Well, they aren't here yet, right? I don't have much time, and well, Gretchen," he said her name, voice dropping even lower, and she shivered in response. "I would really love it if you could take care of me."

"Uh, I'm not sure-"

"Please?"

Shit. He'd used the magic word. Gretchen was a sucker for a softly spoken *please*. She cleared her throat and nodded. Part of her was jumping up and down with excitement.

*Heck yeah, she could take care of him. All. Night. Long.*

*Eeek! No. Bad girl.*

Now was not the time for naughty bedroom thoughts. She had a head of hair to save and a face to uncover underneath all that scratchy scruff. She didn't mind facial hair on a man, but this guy's beard and mustache needed to be taken in hand. As in, it needed to go.

"Okay, well if you insist," she replied and walked back over to where she'd sat him down.

"Thank you," he said, flashing a panty-melting grin her way.

*Day-yum.*

His smile should come with a warning label, she thought as she readjusted the cape around his neck when she realized it was cutting into his skin. She unsnapped it, then redid it on a larger setting.

Or tried to anyway. Sheesh, he had a really thick neck.

"Is that too tight?"

"No, it's okay," he said, and seemed to purr as she ran her hands through his hair.

"*Hmm.* I can see you washed it this morning, but

I'd like to go over it again, if that is alright? I have some great products that would work wonders with hair as thick as yours."

She spun the chair around and tipped it back, turning on the water from the specialty sinks she'd had replaced. Then Gretchen proceeded to build a good lather in his hair with some of the special avocado oil and mint shampoo she'd decided to carry.

The product line was very good, in her humble opinion. It was new and sulfate-free. The owner boasted only the best organic ingredients, and the scents were out of this world. Gretchen was hooked.

Her sexy new client seemed to watch her every move with blue eyes dark as midnight. She caught her breath, lost in the fathomless and faintly glowing orbs. They were almost magical, she thought, shaking her head to clear it.

Gretchen swallowed hard and cleared her throat. Just great, she thought. The fucker was so damn hot, now she was seeing things that weren't there.

"*Oof,*" she bumped her hip on the sink and grimaced.

"You okay?" his concern unsettled her.

*Darn it.*

He was making her nervous. Gretchen was

tempted to put soap in his eye just to get a break from that steady stare of his. Well, maybe some chit-chat would break the tension.

"Fine. Am I hurting you? Or is the chair uncomfortable?" she asked when she couldn't take it anymore.

"Not at all. Why do you ask?"

"Well, you keep watching me like I'm going to make a mistake and get soap in your eye or something."

"That's not why I'm watching you, Gretchen," he said, using her full name and making it sound sexier than she'd ever thought it could. "I just like the way you move."

"Who me?" she asked.

"Yes, you," he replied without hesitation.

His eyes flashed like blue lightning. The heat inside of them visible and Gretchen felt it all the way to her toes. Clearly, there was some physical chemistry going on here. She went back to his hair, trying to ignore him.

"I apologize if I made you self-conscious, but I can't seem to stop staring. You're really something else," he murmured and seemed to be serious.

In a weak moment of self-doubt, Gretchen

wondered if he were poking fun. Or worse, maybe someone put him up to it. She frowned.

"It's okay. You're not bothering me," she fibbed, deciding to change the subject. "You know, you could really use a shave as well as a haircut. Did you burn yourself smoking or something?" she asked, running her hands over a patch that looked as if it were singed off.

"Uh, I don't smoke. But yes, you're right. Do you offer full service for men?"

"I do. Did you want full service?" she asked, and felt her blush spread across her cheeks at the innuendo.

Of course, that wasn't what he meant. She finished rinsing his hair and towel dried it, pulling the seat into an upright position before leading him to her workstation.

He walked closely behind her, a little closer than was usual for her clients, but she remained calm. Or tried to. Truth was, he made the hair on the back of her neck stand up, and she wondered what it was he was playing at. Men like him didn't usually stare at girls like her.

"Why, yes, Gretchen. I'd like that very much."

"Okay then, I'd be happy to give you a cut and a

shave," she said with a tight smile. "So, is there anything you want done in particular?"

He sat down easily, watching her from the mirror, and Gretchen's whole body felt as if he'd stroked it with those long fingers of his. Yeah, she had noticed them. There was just something about a man's hands that spoke to her. He had great hands.

They were solid and big, rough, but not careless. She wondered what it would feel like if he touched her with intent with those big man's hands of his.

Short, blunt nails topped each finger. They were surprisingly clean, cuticles and all. Gretchen could almost imagine the way they would tease and caress her most secret places. Her girly bits tingled, as if her whole body was blushing with awareness.

*Did it just get really hot in here?*

Gretchen tried not to stare as she adjusted the height of the chair. Hell, what good was not staring when he smelled better than a tray of double fudge brownies?

Whatever soap he used, she would swear there were hints of cocoa and vanilla bean. He smelled delicious. *Good enough to nibble,* she thought outrageously.

Her cheeks heated, and she knew she was

blushing for real now. Biting her lip, she scolded herself. That was no way to think of a client.

It was time to get to work and stop this ridiculous fantasy of hers. She took his head in her hands and straightened it, using her fingers to brush back his rich, dark locks. With his hair combed out of the way, she finally got a good look at his face.

*Dayum.*

Reg Cray, whoever he was, was hot. Like really hot. Like really, really, someone get a fire extinguisher hot. When she was a teenager, she recalled crushing on movie and rock stars, but Reg was even better looking than them.

His nose was long and straight, but not too big. It fit his chiseled features, accented by his sharp cheekbones and a square jaw. His skin was tanned from the sun, like a golden honey color, but she could tell he was fair in winter. That hair of his was the real clincher though. His dark brown mop was unruly, but even that could not disguise the thick and glossy layers to his mane.

She wondered if he had any Latin or Italian blood. He must have to give him such gorgeous coloring. Her favorite feature were his eyes.

*Lawd, have mercy.*

Dark and glittering, his gorgeous eyes sparkled

out at her through thick black lashes, like sapphires on a velvet swatch. Bedroom eyes if she ever saw a pair.

*Beautiful. Sexy too.*

There was no doubt about it. This guy was completely out of her league. Depressing as the thought was, it allowed her to focus as she lifted her comb and began creating sections out of the long tresses.

"Now, what has you making such a sad face, Gretchen? My hair can't be that bad, can it?" he asked, joking with her. Gretchen lifted her head up and met his unwavering stare in the mirror.

"What? Oh, no, sorry, it's nothing," she replied, and smiled tightly. She went back to paying attention to what she was doing.

*More hair, less stare.*

There was no reason on earth for her thoughts to turn so personal. He was a client, not a potential hubby on her own personal version of *the Bachelor.*

"Okay, here is what I have in mind," she talked, wanting his approval while she began trimming his locks with a scissor at first.

"You can do anything you want to me," Reg said, eyes glowing.

A shiver ran through her. If only he knew what she wanted to do, she thought wickedly.

"You got it," Gretchen replied, lifting her trimmer.

Last, she'd use a straight razor, but she'd wait to show him her skill with the blade. Concentrating was a bitch, but she'd get through it.

He was just a man, for fuck's sake. A cute man, but a stranger, and more importantly, a *customer*.

That was all he was to her. Nothing special. Not fate or kismet. Just a client.

*Liar,* her inner voice whispered in her head and Gretchen almost dropped her shears.

That voice in her head could be such a heifer sometimes. She cleared her throat and got back to work, when she was done, Reginald Cray was going to look like a million dollars.

*And then what?* She wondered to herself. Of course, inner Gretchen had an answer.

*Lick him. Then hang a sign around his neck that says property of Gretchen Kaepernick.*

A frustrated sigh escaped her lips. She really needed to get laid if she was going to fantasize about every man who walked into her salon.

*Not every man,* inner her replied. *Just him.*

Fucking fuck. It was gonna be a long day.

# Chapter Seven

By the time she was done cutting the hair on his head, Reg had to admit he looked about a million times better. He would never underestimate the skills of a unisex hairstylist again.

She was an absolute genius. With nimble and efficient swipes of her shears, Gretchen had cut and groomed his unruly locks to perfection. She'd shaved the sides and back all the way to the skin on his scalp. Leaving the top long enough to reach his chin.

He'd never have dared go so short on his own, but he had to admit, he loved it. It revealed the tattoo on the back of his neck, making it look even better in his opinion. His regular barber, Lou, was old school.

Everyone pretty much got the same fade, but Gretchen here gave him an edge with this style haircut. She'd made him look good in a way that was reminiscent of modern soccer players everywhere. He kinda dug the sport.

Especially, after Hunter had organized an in-Pride version of the World Cup last summer. It was awesome, and Reg's team had won with a single glorious goal made by Mikey in the last ninety seconds of the match. Brayden, who'd played goalkeeper for the opposing team, had been super pissed.

*Good times,* he smirked. He was more focused on the present, which was much more interesting in his opinion, than on replaying that soccer match in his head.

The ever lovely Gretchen was running her hands through his hair again and the platonic contact shot straight to his dick. Thank fuck the cape he wore covered that part of him.

She seemed to like the length on top and was busy focusing on the thick and long hair, pulling it forward in glossy waves. Thankfully, she didn't leave them there. He'd worried at first that he was going to get itchy with his hair in his face, but he hadn't wanted to offend her.

He'd fucking glue it there if she wanted him to,

but the sexy woman seemed to sense that. Watching his reaction in the mirror, she smirked and used a little product then tossed the thick waves back off his forehead. He liked that even better.

Every time she moved her fingers through his hair, he got a whiff of her intoxicating scent. His Tiger, ever present, was surer than he'd ever been since he first set eyes on her that she was meant to be his.

"Now for that beard," Gretchen muttered, moving to stand in front of him.

This female was his fated mate. It was enough to blow his head clean off. He wanted to sing and dance and scream all at the same time. Well, mostly, he wanted to toss her fine ass over his shoulder and run away with her. It was a near thing.

She was so close, right there, scant inches away, and yet, she didn't seem to be affected at all.

Sure, Reg had expected to be mated to a Shifter, but maybe that was prejudiced of him. Elissa had been a human before the Puspa, and he assumed Gretchen was too, but maybe he was wrong.

Could she be descended from a line of Witches? He would have guessed she was something magical, for sure, just by the way she seemed to have him mesmerized. But so far, he'd been unable to identify exactly what if any supernatural heritage, the little vixen had in her blood line.

He blamed it on the styling products and cleaning solutions that were thick in the air. Worse now that more people surrounded them. After she'd shampooed and conditioned his hair, her staff had started to arrive. They made the introduction and went to work cleaning and getting their stations ready.

After that, a steady stream of clients had signed in and were waiting their turns patiently, using the time to gossip and catch up. He'd heard their idle chit chat like a dull buzzing in the background, but his focus was on Gretchen herself.

She was a puzzle. A total mystery to him. One he desperately wanted to solve. Reg needed to. He just had to know everything about her.

"I'm sorry to keep you waiting," she apologized, returning after stopping to show one of the new employees how to use the credit card machine.

His sweet Gretchen, whatever she was, was not only gorgeous, he realized, but she was smart and funny. A real people person and terrific with her employees who seemed to warm to her immediately.

"No really, thank you for being so sweet," she said, and he wanted to yowl in pleasure.

*She thinks I'm sweet. How about that?!*

"I can't tell you how embarrassed I am at the amount of times I've had to stop. If you like, I can have one of the other stylists finish the job," she started.

*Hell to the no.*

There was only one person he wanted touching his hair, his face, *any part of him*, and that was her.

"Thank you for offering, *shona*. But no, I'll wait for you. However long it takes," he murmured.

She cocked her head and nodded at him. The term of endearment familiar to his kind, had accidentally slipped from his tongue. He couldn't take it back now. Fuck that. He did not want to take it back.

She was his *shona*. His sweetheart. The one bright spot in his life.

*Yes*, his heart squeezed in his chest at the acknowledgement.

Gretchen was his whole heart. She just didn't know it yet. He waited, albeit impatiently, until she came back with a dish of shaving butter and a hot towel in her hands. She used the clipper to trim down the uneven mess that was his beard first. Then, she wrapped the hot towel on his face and mixed the butter to a froth.

He watched as she sharpened a straight-edged

razor the old fashioned way, and he was immediately impressed. Gretchen removed the towel, standing in front of him, leaning over to reach his skin as she applied the foam to his cheeks, chin, and neck.

Fucking hell. He was going to go off like a volcano at her unwittingly provocative display. Gretchen held the razor up. For a moment, he wondered if this was a good idea, cocking her head to the side as if trying to find the right angle.

"Excuse me," she muttered, cheeks going pink as she tapped his knees.

Reg could hardly stop the low purr in his throat as he moved his knees apart, allowing the slip of a woman to move between them.

"There we go," she whispered, spreading more frothy cream on his upper lip.

Reg held still. It was all he could do while that certain part of him hardened like a steel rod. The damn thing was throbbing, aching so for her. Hell, it threatened to burst through his pants.

*Fuck. This is not a good idea.* He thought, but the Tiger disagreed.

*Oh, yes, it is. A very good idea. Mine.*

Reg had to work doubly hard to push the beast back. His Tiger had identified her as his fated mate and now the beast wanted him to claim the feisty beauty. He just needed to wait for the right time to talk to her.

Gretchen studied him, leaning forward ever so slightly. Her bountiful breasts rustled the fabric of his cape, and he shuddered at the almost contact.

"Cold?"

"Uh, no."

"Okay. Hold still," she whispered.

Reg inhaled, the foamy mixture smelled of peppermint, and some other woodsy spice he couldn't name. It was light, and pleasant, but he wished it was unscented. He'd much rather get another lungful of her.

"Damn, Gretch, you give that close a shave to everyone? Cause then I'm next, girl," Marion, a friendly thirty-something male with thick-rimmed glasses and spiky black hair called out.

He was one of her new stylists, and had introduced himself as *Marion the Gay Blade*, a tribute to his favorite Zorro movie, he'd said while holding up his rainbow colored scissors. Reg went to look at the male, a snarl on his lips, but Gretchen held him still.

"Don't move," she chided, grinning at her new worker's shenanigans. "Hey, Marion, your poster is falling," she told the male who shrieked and went to apply more tack to the back of his ten by ten image of the movie in question.

"Now, George, you stay put, honey, you know I need you," he told the image of George Hamilton dressed in an avocado green Zorro costume.

Normally, Reg would have laughed his ass off. He liked that classic film. But for some reason, his first instinct had him wanting to tear the fucker's head off.

Jealousy was a new emotion for him. One he wasn't sure he liked. He knew Shifters tended to be possessive when they found their mates, but he hadn't truly understood the sensation until just then. After all, he'd never wanted to claim anyone before her.

*Mine. Mate.*

"Okay, now, I have a straight razor against your throat, no sudden moves, got it?" she commanded.

"Yes ma'am," his lips twitched, but he didn't dare grin.

Gretchen narrowed her baby blues, so different from his own dark eyes, as she started to move the cold metal against his overheated skin. Oh yeah, Reg had a fever alright, and there was only one cure for it. Her.

Corny, but true. He needed her badly. His Tiger

chuffed at the way she ordered him to stay still, the beast enjoying her bossy side. He'd never liked dominant women before, but if she wanted to tell him what to do, he was game.

It was pretty damn sexy. She moved with the same quick, efficient strokes against his face as she had his hair. Wielding the razor expertly, she didn't nick him once. Not even a little.

"There, all done," she said, and pulled back way too soon for his liking. She quickly returned, thank fuck, and wiped away the remaining shave butter with a warm, damp towel.

Next, she splashed a little aftershave on his skin that made him tingle. Or was that her?

"I mix this myself with some essential oils that are good for tightening pores and nourishing the skin," she said.

"That's good," he muttered, not really sure what the hell he was saying. He just wanted her to never stop petting him like that.

She pursed her lips, trying not to grin, and he noticed the cutest little dimple at the corner of her mouth. Totally kissable. He couldn't wait to test that theory himself.

She was talking again though, and he brought his attention back to her. Nodding as if he had any clue what she'd been saying. Not like he could just admit he'd gotten side-tracked with thoughts of kissing her mouth, her breasts, *fuck*, everywhere. There he went again. Reg was having a difficult time keeping his one track mind out of the gutter.

"It's completely natural with bergamot, peppermint, and eucalyptus essential oils. All great for healing, and moisturizing the skin," she explained as she rubbed the oil onto his neck and face.

*Dear gods*, if she didn't stop touching him, he'd never be able to stand up again.

Might as well accept the fact he was going to have to live with a permanent hardon until he found a moment to speak to her about their situation. But how did he go about that exactly?

"Okay, so, just meet me at the counter when you're ready, and I will ring you up," she said, and unsnapped the cape, shaking the stray hair onto the floor.

She spun around grabbing the broom and swept the floor around the chair. Reg stood up and rearranged his t-shirt, making sure to drape over the obvious bulge in his pants.

Hopefully, he did it in time to save himself some embarrassment. Of course, Marion had turned at that very moment and winked at him. Reg just shook his head.

Gretchen was already finished, placing the broom and dustpan against the wall as she handed him a piece of paper with the price of the haircut and shave scrawled across it. He reached into his back pocket for his wallet and waited until she was looking at him to take the plunge.

"Hey, uh, Gretchen?"

"Yeah?"

"Uh, I was wondering if you would go out with me, like tonight," he blurted as she ran his credit card through the machine.

"Excuse me?" she asked, pausing with his card in her hand. Her baby blues were open wide, and her plump pink lips parted slightly.

She looked so fucking sexy. He wanted to reach over, grab her by the face and kiss the fuck out of her until they were both panting with need.

"Sorry, I---"

"No, it's me. You see, I'm trying to ask you out and doing a bad job of it, I guess. But what do you say?"

Reg rubbed the back of his neck.

"Wait, what?"

"You? Me? Food?"

"Uh…"

"Come out with me, Gretchen. Have dinner with me tonight," he said, finally.

Seconds passed, and when she still hadn't responded, Reg began to grow uncomfortable. Hell, his heart was liable to pound him to death in the interim.

*"Gretchen, answer that giant man before I do,"* Marion hissed, clearly listening in on them.

"Shh," she snapped at him, before turning to Reg. *"You* want to take *me* out on a date?" she echoed.

"Damn, boss lady, you are quick. You sure are," Marion replied, rolling his heavily made-up eyes.

He walked over to where Gretchen was standing behind the counter and took the credit card from her hand since she seemed to have forgotten it.

At first, Reg wasn't so happy about the way the guy was loud and flirty, but he recognized it as playful banter. He was funny and was obviously a friend.

"There you go, Mr. Cray. Sign here. Now, boss lady, you just say yes now so this sexy man can leave, and get on with his day," Marion replied and winked at Reg. He also whistled wolfishly, looking reg up and down and shaking his head. Reg blushed at the appraisal, hoping he made the grade.

"Yeah, say yes, Gretchen," Reg added, nodding in agreement.

He grinned wickedly at the object of his affections, liking the way she seemed surprised by his question. Reg didn't mind being admired by Marion or anyone else, but his focus was on Gretchen. He wanted her approval and hers alone. A pink blush crept across her cheeks and his heart raced at the sight.

*Damn,* she was pretty.

"Um, okay, yeah, sure," she finally agreed.

"Great. I'll pick you up tonight at 8. Is that alright?"

"Yes," Marion prompted.

"Um, yeah that is fine. We close at 7, so 8 is good. I live upstairs, the entrance is right on the side of the salon," she said and pointed.

"Fantastic, I'll see you then," Reg replied, reaching out to touch her hand gently. He smiled and let go reluctantly.

"Alright," she said and waved goodbye.

Once he was outside, in the brisk spring air, doubt began to set in. Holy crap. Reg had a date with the most important woman in the entire world.

She was to him, at any rate.

*Gretchen Kaepernick,* he bit his lip as he played her

name in his mind over and over again, picturing her curvy, petite frame, and her fascinating baby blue eyes. Finally, he'd found his one true mate. The person he was destined to be with forever.

*Gulp.*

He couldn't afford to fuck this up. Reg needed a strategy. A surefire way to woo his mate. A perfect plan to trap her in his more than willing arms for all time.

*Yes, we need to set the purrfect trap,* his Tiger agreed.

As a hunter, the animal inside him appreciated this line of thinking. Now he just had to execute it.

*Grrr.*

# Chapter Eight

"Excuse me, Neta? Can I speak with you?"

Reg knocked on Hunter's office door. The Maverick Pride was smaller than most Shifter Groups, especially the Wolf Packs who seemed to breed like rabbits in Reg's opinion. But they had something special there in Maverick Point and he knew it. Fuck, he still could not believe he had almost fucked it up.

The Maverick Pride House was not only where the Neta and Nari lived and spent much of their time, but it was a place that all the Tigers within the Pride could access.

The private dwelling of the Alpha family, and the members of the Tiger Guard who lived there, were not open for tours, of course. But it was understood that this was a haven for them all.

Hunter prided himself on his easy accessibility to his Pride, and though Reg was still feeling his way, he knew the Neta would welcome his questions. Reg waited until the powerful Alpha Tiger's voice boomed from inside.

"Come in, Reg," he called, scenting Reg from inside.

Sitting behind his desk with his mate perched on his lap, Hunter looked Reg in the eye until the younger man looked away. The man's naturally dominant Tiger demanded submission from every single Tiger in his Pride. Reg was no fool. He would never challenge his Neta. He averted his gaze and bared his throat in a sign of willing submission to the man's power and rank.

In the wild, tigers were solitary creatures, but in the Shifter world, being alone usually meant being unstable. Shifters needed social bonds. That was why Tiger Prides, Wolf Packs, Rabbit Fluffles, Bear Clans, and more existed. Plus all the groups for supernatural creatures other than Shifters. Like Witch Covens and Fairy Circles.

Humans ignored or pretended not to notice the paranormal world, but that mattered very little either way. Shifters, like other supes, existed. In fact, they thrived right alongside normals. Keeping *the secret* was tantamount. It was the single most important rule in the supernatural handbook.

Normals could not handle knowing supernaturals existed without trying to harness and take power they could not possibly understand. Anyway, supes were much better at policing their own than with interference from outsiders.

Reg understood the importance of having a strong leader and a good Pride. He couldn't have picked a better man than Hunter Maverick as Neta. On two legs, the man was as strong as any beast, and as for in his fur, well, Hunter's Tiger was almost half again the size of the next largest one in the Pride.

All that power and strength still wasn't enough to rule a group of Shifters whose instincts ran high when it came to aggression, fighting, mating, all the above.

Hunter was a fantastic Neta because along with all of his great strength came a tremendous amount of patience and compassion for his Pride mates. They were lucky to have him, and Reg knew it.

"Sit down." Hunter nodded, holding his cherished mate in his arms.

"Hello, Reg," Elissa said, smiling sweetly.

She looked as if she had just been thoroughly kissed, but Reg was careful not to gaze too long. Not that he wanted too. While happy for them, it had all the ick factor of catching his parents making out.

*So gross.*

And the cause for some heavy talks with his guidance counselor in high school after he'd caught Mom riding Dad like a rodeo cowgirl on more than one occasion. Why he was always the one to walk in on them and not Robbie, his brother, he didn't fucking know. Just his luck, he supposed.

"Um, hey," Reg began, not noticing the third person in the room until the old Witch turned his electric blue gaze on him.

Magic hummed in the air, but Reg was careful not to react. Uncle Uzzi was the last person he wanted to rub wrong, especially when an idea hit him. That sly old Witch had sent him for that haircut. He must have known all along his mate was waiting for him there.

"Well, Reginald Cray, that is an improvement."

"Uncle Uzzi," he said, Tiger peeking through his eyes to survey the elderly Witch.

"Your haircut. It suits you, Reg," Uncle Uzzi smiled broadly from his perch on one of the large wing chairs to the side of Hunter's desk.

"Oh, yeah, thanks, Uncle Uzzi."

"Of course," the sly old man said, looking down at his fingernails after buffing them on his white sweater. "So, tell me, did anything interesting happen while you were there?"

Uncle Uzzi asked innocently enough, but Reg noticed the mated Alpha couple trying hard not to smile. He knew it! This was all a plot. He should feel angry, pissed, something. But he couldn't. Fact was, Reg was so deeply pleased, he could only smile in response.

"So, you know already," Reg told the room at large.

"Well? Are you going to be a bore, or will you confirm our suspicions about you and a certain new salon owner?" Uncle Uzzi let out an exasperated sigh.

"I can see there is no point in denying it," he smiled and addressed all three of them. "Gretchen is my fated mate, and I have a date with her tonight."

"Wonderful!"

"That's great, Reg," Hunter's voice was the deepest, and therefore easiest to pick out.

"Um, I came here because, well, I just needed some help. I don't know anything about her besides she's beautiful, smart, funny, sweet, and damn, she knows her way around a straight-edged razor," he said grinning.

"Um, gee, Reg how romantic?" Elissa said, though it sounded more like a question. "So, what do you want to know?"

"I don't know, everything for starters, but really, I wanna know where to take her. What does she like to eat? Where is she comfortable? I want tonight to be special."

"Oh, well, Gretchen is pretty easygoing. She likes pretty much everything," Elissa shrugged.

"I heard her say she liked the sandwich Trigger brought them for lunch the other day," Hunter added, shrugging.

"Yes, but what else? I don't wanna fuc-, I mean, mess this up, Nari," he asked, correcting his language when Hunter narrowed his teal eyes.

*Shit.*

Reg knew better than that. He'd come here seeking Hunter and Elissa's advice because nothing had ever mattered this much. Not in his world. His *shona* was everything to him, and he wanted to show her that he cared. That he, Reg Cray, could be the man she needed. Of course, after listening to these three, he was not sure any of their advice was helpful.

"Reg, look at me," Uncle Uzzi insisted. "Gretchen is special. You are right to be concerned about your first date and what impression you will make. But do not lose sight that this is your fated mate you are talking about here. Dinner is great, but unless you already told her, you will need to explain what being mates actually means."

"That's right," Elissa added, frowning. "I can tell you from experience, it is a lot to take in."

"I'm not sure how to do that," Reg confessed. "And no I did not get a chance, you see, the salon was crowded. It was full of a lot of different scents, and I know I should have figured it out, but am I right in thinking she's a *full human?*"

"Yes," Elissa said, and bit her lip nervously.

Her hands were on her swollen belly with Hunter's protectively covering them. Their love was already legend, and Reg knew in his heart that if given the opportunity, his and Gretchen's could rival it. Fuck, he was already halfway head over heels for her.

So, what if she didn't know a thing about Shifters? That wasn't a big deal, right? The Nari had been human too until she'd been bitten by her true mate in a claiming ritual as old as time.

Afterwards, she'd experienced the very rare

*Puspa.* The changing bite only occurred if the Fates permitted. Not every mate was destined for that kind of transformation.

The *Puspa* allowed a normal human to turn into a Shifter. No one knew how or why, but it was considered a very rare and special blessing. A symbol that the two mates were more than just fated, they were written in the stars. The universe had selected them to become stronger and their bonds proved unbreakable.

Reg had been there to witness the Nari's *Puspa,* It was an exceedingly painful process to observe, and his esteem for the petite blonde had risen to new heights.

Elissa was now a Shifter like the rest of them, only she was a rare and unique White Tiger. She'd made the adjustments to Shifter life quite easily, as far as Reg could tell and Hunter was a very lucky man.

"Listen, I'm not really sure how she will take it, Reg, Gretchen doesn't exactly believe in fairy tales," Elissa continued, gnawing at her lip until Hunter stopped it with a short, hard kiss.

"She might not believe at first, Reg. But sometimes in life, there are challenges to be met. Not every mating is easily won, but if you are sure about this and you want her, you have to tell her," Hunter said.

"I want her. There is no one else," Reg confirmed.

"Good! It is important that you explain everything to her before you take any steps towards claiming her. Do you understand?"

Uncle Uzzi narrowed his eyes, and for a moment, Reg felt very much like a cub getting a scolding. His Tiger wasn't at all happy with waiting to claim his mate, but his human side understood the need for it.

After their brief discussion, Reg headed back to his room to devise his plan. He would take her out for a good meal. *Cliff's Steakhouse* served divine meals with prime organically raised beef and amazing side dishes all locally sourced. It was expensive and exclusive.

*Purrfect* for his one of a kind mate. Afterwards, he'd take her for a drive or a walk in the park. They could talk, maybe hold hands, and if he was really fucking lucky, he'd get to kiss her sweet, pouty lips.

His cock stiffened, and he growled deep in his throat. What was the female doing to him? Just thinking about the possibility of touching her had his Tiger scratching at his skin and his cock ready to hammer nails through wood.

He could not go to her like this, he'd attack her

before she could even say hello. The thought of her calling the cops on his ass was not appealing. Reg needed to blow off some steam. Jerking off held no appeal, but a run might do it.

Excellent idea! He could take to his fur and race through the woods. That should wear off some of his excess energy before seeing her. It was a great way to calm the beast inside him.

Reg left his clothes in the open shed behind the Pride House and shifted into his animal. A familiar magical hum washed over him, and he felt bones break, muscles bend, and fur sprout along his sensitized skin. The process was painful, but tolerable with practice. It only took about forty-five seconds all in all.

His Tiger was a deep orange with thick black markings on his shoulders and back. He stood still, growling as he wrestled control from the animal. Reg did not expect his Tiger's need for his mate would be so powerful. It was almost too strong, but he managed to rein him in with promises of what was to come later.

As he stalked through the budding Springtime forest, Reg felt another presence. As if someone were watching him. He sniffed and panted, tasting the air.

A female had travelled through the woods not long before him. He ignored the scent after cataloging it.

Pride members were allowed to roam the acres of forest surrounding the Pride House. The land was legally owned by Hunter's corporation, Maverick Development. Typically, he would go and search out the visiting Pride mate, but he had no desire for company.

Especially not female company. He picked up his pace, running over roots and rocks until he was sweating and out of breath. Eventually, he scaled a tall oak tree just to lie out on one of its sturdier branches. There, Reg basked in the sun and pictured the upcoming night.

Dinner with his mate. Nerves rose while he imagined picking her up and taking her to the ritzy little restaurant. He wanted to feed her, to please her, to show her he would be a good mate.

After a good long while, Reg headed back and switched his fur for skin in the grass behind the shed where he'd left his clothes.

"Oh, my, my, how we have grown."

"Well, well. Hello there, Reg."

Two Pride females were lounging against the shed, spying it would seem, and perusing Reg as he shifted back to human like they were starving, and he was a full course meal.

Bad etiquette, to say the least. Shifters knew better than to stare uninvited. His Tiger snarled and Reg tugged on his pants. It was not good form to stare at the naked body of someone who'd just shifted.

Usually, said person was antsy, their senses heightened and a bit angry after the sometimes painful process. He sure as fuck did not want any female looking at him naked except for Gretchen. Hers were the only pair of eyes he wanted feasting on his form.

"What do you want?" he snapped, not liking the snarky smirk on either female's face.

"We don't *want* anything, Reg. Unless you do, of course," the blonde purred.

"Can't we appreciate one of our Pride's most trusted guards?" asked the brown-haired female.

"Anyway, I was wondering if maybe you'd like to come over tonight. I have something I'd love for you to try on," the former added, striking what was supposed to be a seductive pose.

Unfortunately for her, Reg had never been so turned off. The thinner one stalked forward in what he assumed she thought was a sexy walk. He turned his face, the scent of her hairspray overwhelming. It was all he could do not to sneeze.

"No thanks, ladies. And just a tip, but you would do well to avoid asking me in the future. I am no longer on the market," he said, and started to walk away only to be stopped by the female's hand on his arm.

His Tiger roared inside his mind's eye, and it was all he could do not to push the woman off of him. He would never ever strike a woman, but her nails biting into his skin was really pissing him off. His Tiger wanted no one's hands on him except his mate's.

"What? You're turning us down?" the brunette barked the question.

"Ha! A traitor like you can't have many prospects, Reginald Cray, you should take what I am offering," she frowned hard at him, her smile turned into a sneer.

"Excuse me? I am one of the Nari's own trusted guards, not a traitor. Now, I suggest you leave the Pride House until you can remember your manners," Reginald said and straightened his shoulders.

Dominant women were not usually a problem, but something was not right about how these women were behaving. He could be reacting to having found his mate, but Reg felt it was more than that. Not liking to roar at females, he could not control the growl in his voice as he glared at them and opened his mouth once more.

"Leave. Now. Before I report you both to the Nari," he told them.

As Alpha fem, part of Elissa's job was to maintain control of the females in their Pride. Female Tiger Shifters, like all Big Cats, experienced a heat cycle which could make them agitated. If that were the issue here, he had a duty to arrange help.

He could scent nothing different about the women. Only anger and spite. But Reg was no expert in the matter. He would leave that to the Nari, making a mental note to speak to her.

"You hear that Pam, he's going to report us," snorted the taller woman. "I know what you are, Reginald Cray," she said, stepping closer. "Maybe you need a reminder."

"I said *go*," Reg snarled, no longer able to deny his beast's anger.

The force of his roar shook the very ground, and the two females ran off. He'd recognized both of them but had never dated or slept with either woman. Their claims to know him were completely false. Even when he'd been stupid enough to believe

Blake, he had never hung around with the man's women.

And yes, Reg recognized them from the past as hanging around the ex-Beta inside the Pride House on occasion. Blake had worked his way through many of the Pride females, but not Reg. He'd had very little to do with them.

Reg was a firm believer in not shitting where he ate. He'd always kept his dating brief and outside of Maverick Point, not wanting the hassle of awkward encounters after the fact.

Plus, he'd always been a dreamer. Even as a young man, Reg had wanted to believe he had a fated mate. How could he face her within the Pride if he'd slept with everyone they would be living and working with? He might not be the smartest guy around, but he was glad he'd had the foresight to curb his lusty appetites to women outside their town.

Luckily, his mate was nothing like those two females. Gretchen was beautiful, ambitious, funny, sweet, and smart. There was so much he wanted to know about her, and he couldn't wait to woo her properly.

Shifters knew with no doubts their mates were their one and only, but Gretchen was human. She would need time and convincing, Reg nodded to himself, more than ready for the challenge. He pushed the encounter with the two skinny females out of his mind and went to get ready for his mate.

Anticipation of what was to come made him nervous, but Reg was okay with nerves. It was only natural. This was the rest of his life on the line here.

Both he and his Tiger were up for this, he just had to keep his eye on the target. Nothing was as important as claiming Gretchen.

*Nothing.*

*Grrrrrrr.*

*Mine.*

# Chapter Nine

Gretchen was so nervous she didn't know what to do. After fixing her hair for the tenth time, she finally pulled on a pair of sling-back pumps and readjusted the flattering wrap-around dress she'd splurged on from *Jessica's Closet*.

She'd run over to the awesome boutique located next to her salon right before closing time and found the pretty flower printed dress almost instantly. Shopping was always like that for her.

Gretchen seemed to know within ten minutes of being inside a shop whether she was going to find anything she liked. It was usually a matter of them not having her size, but Jessica specialized in dressing women with larger assets in styles that were both fun and flirty.

Thank heaven! She was just so tired of department stores that only seemed to carry trendy clothing for thinner women. So called plus-sized outfits tended to be ugly as sin or made for an older crowd.

Gretchen was in her prime. Her thirties were still young enough to want to dress a certain way that did not remind her of her bitchy aunt's old as fuck living room furniture. And no, it didn't make her a slut, *fuck you very much.*

She just didn't want to wear clothing that suggested she was ready for a home! Gretchen had always been larger than average, and it had taken a little while for her to embrace her fuller figure. Moving to Maverick Point was turning out to be the best decision she'd made in a long while, if for the shopping alone.

Relieved she wouldn't have to limit her shopping to online stores in order to find the right sizes and styles, Gretchen sighed happily as she looked herself over. She loved the way her new dress clung to her curves, making her feel pretty and feminine.

Satisfied with how she looked, she sat down at her tidy kitchen counter and rapped her newly manicured fingernails on the white and blue tiles. She could not believe she'd scored a date on her opening day. Yes. she had planned to celebrate with a small bottle of champagne by herself, but this was so much better.

She huffed out a breath, biting her lower lip. Gretchen was so dang nervous, she could not sit still. What was happening to her? She'd never felt this out of whack over a date.

Then again, it wasn't every day a man who looked like a cover model asked her out. She closed her eyes, and his face was there, those gorgeous, chiseled features, sinfully plump lips, and midnight blue eyes boring into hers. She pictured Reg Cray as if he were standing in front of her. His face practically burned into her memory.

True, Reg was beyond her sphere of experience, but it was more than his looks that had her heart doing cartwheels inside her chest. There was just something about him that made her want to climb on top of him and not let go until they were both sweaty and panting. He had all the makings of a man who could rock her world, and for the first time in her life, Gretchen was sorely tempted to let him prove it.

*Yum.*

Those were some pretty intense feelings for a guy she'd only just met. Gretchen had boyfriends before. She was not a virgin, not by a longshot. But something about that steady midnight gaze of his had her body trembling with need.

Maybe this last dry spell was too damn long. When was the last time she'd gone on a date? And actually had a good time?

Anxious and excited, she wondered if maybe she was putting too many expectations on this thing. It was just dinner. A good-looking man like that must have a list a mile long of ready and willing women. Hell, he'd probably asked her out to just be sociable.

Gretchen rolled her shoulders and exhaled a deep breath. This was ridiculous. There was absolutely no reason for her to feel so antsy. Instead of focusing on her ridiculous case of nerves, she forced her mind to think over the happenings of the day.

*Cut it Out* had been so busy. And not just with clients who had booked appointments beforehand, but they'd had walk-ins and folks wanting to check out the shop all day. Some were prior customers of her new employees, and others were just folks who wanted to say hello.

The phone never seemed to stop ringing, and she'd booked appointments for what seemed like the next two months in advance. It was more than she'd ever hoped for.

Her two new hires, Marion, and Bonnie, proved to be invaluable workers who'd brought their own clients with them. That was always a plus. She'd met them beforehand and knew immediately they would make excellent employees.

Gretchen had a gift for easing people. It came from working with so many over the past ten years. People really let the tea flow when they were getting their hair done. Like bartending, it was one of those jobs where you were part stylist and part therapist.

She did not mind. Gretchen loved people, and her outgoing nature made her easy to talk to. It was a blessing, she supposed, and she was going to take it as such.

Bonnie was the quieter of the two new stylists, with her long blonde hair tied back in a neat braid. Her clientele were mostly older women, but they seemed to love her, and Gretchen approved.

Marion, on the other hand, was loud and flamboyant. His customers were younger, a lot of men, and teenagers who liked his colorful and modern approach to cutting and styling hair. The man was a whiz when it came to highlights. She'd watch him foil two heads of hair like nobody's business. Hell, even she did not work that quickly.

The two opposites worked extremely well together, and with Gretchen managing everyone, they did just beautifully for their first day.

She'd even found a third stylist, and she'd hired two young women who were qualified to do nails as well. For a small town, Maverick Point had a ton of people who seemed to rejoice in her opening. Things were going to go very well, she thought with an excited squeal.

It seemed after Mrs. Bowers had closed up shop, the townspeople had had to travel all the way to the shopping mall to get their hair and nails done. There was a barbershop in town, but Lou was currently out visiting his grandchildren, and the gossip was he wanted to move to South Florida.

Either way, people were happy to not have to trek all the way to the busy shopping center for a haircut. A few customers asked about spa treatments, and Gretchen already had a menu of items she was going to add to her growing list of specialties.

Hair treatments, facials, waxing, threading, massage, and more. But that was for another day.

Tonight, she was ready to celebrate her success

by going out with a sexy as sin man who seemed genuinely interested in spending the evening with her. Who knew? Maybe that dry spell would end with a very long overdue night of sexy fun times.

Heck, she wouldn't mind christening her new bed with him.

*Wouldn't that be something?*

*New salon? Check.*

*New apartment? Check.*

*Mind-blowing sex with a willing stud? Check check!*

Gretchen jumped guiltily, face heating at getting caught with those naughty little thoughts running through her head, at the sound of her doorbell ringing. Fucking hell, that was loud! Or maybe it was the fact her apartment was super quiet at the moment.

After she'd closed for the day, Marion and Bonnie had helped her tidy things before leaving, but once they had gone, she was the only person remaining in the whole building. Was a bit lonely, to be honest.

"Coming!" she yelled and immediately blushed at the thought.

Well, with any luck she would be. And soon.

"Hello," she smiled, using the new doorbell camera to see her guest.

It was him, she thought excitedly, and buzzed her

date inside. Gretchen's heart beat double time as Reg climbed the stairs to her apartment in record speed. She opened the door, staring helplessly as he stood there grinning at her like the Cheshire Cat.

"For you," he said, holding out a beautiful bouquet of flowers towards her.

"Oh my! These are my favorite," Gretchen replied, taking them, and pressing the bouquet to her nose. "They're beautiful!" She laughed and accepted the colorful arrangement.

"Your favorite? Mine too."

"Really? I just love tiger lilies. Actually, I just love tigers in general," she confessed, laughing a little self-consciously as she let him into her apartment.

There was an obvious tiger motif in the striped pillows tossed on the couch and the several hand-carved statuettes she had on the shelves. Gretchen had always admired the powerful beasts. Naturally, she liked the flowers named after them.

"You do?" Reg's perfect eyebrows arched over his intense midnight blue eyes.

Damn, he was sexy.

"Yeah, I know it probably sounds corny---"

"Not at all. I think it's amazing," he replied, cutting her off. "Everything about you is amazing," he said, backing her into the room, and she could have sworn his deep blues glowed for a second.

*Must be a trick of the light*, she thought as she turned towards the kitchen.

"Just let me put these in water," she murmured, hyperaware of the electrical currents zipping between them.

"Hey, you read a lot?" he asked, eyes roaming over the apartment to her bookshelves.

"Yeah, sometimes. I love fantasy romance," she confessed, aware of the man like she'd been for no one else.

Reg was so big, and good looking. She wondered for a second what he was doing with someone like her but pushed the thought away hastily. Gretchen was not going to go down that road of insecurity and doubt. She'd worked too hard to get where she was, and she was a fun, bright, and good person.

*Any man was lucky to date her*, she thought with a reassuring nod.

"Did you want this? It might get cold later," Reg said, appearing directly behind her.

Fuck. He smelled so good. Like spice and man, she thought, fighting arousal as her stomach clenched in need. He handed her the light pashmina and clutch she'd left on the couch, his fingers grazing hers as she took them.

"Thank you," she murmured.

"My pleasure," he replied, leaning down and, wait, was he sniffing her?

She must have imagined that. Reg took a step back and ran his hand over the sides of his hair that she'd shaved earlier that day.

"Shall we go?" Gretchen asked, unable to stop the thrill that coursed through her when she looked at him.

*What she wouldn't give for a night in this man's arms! Sigh.*

"Absolutely," he answered, and held his hand out.

She accepted it, shivering slightly at the contact. Christ, he was warm! In fact, heat seemed to emanate from his entire body as he walked behind her down the stairs, one hand on her back.

Gretchen felt the effect ripple through her, all the way to her toes. Ever the gentleman, Reg escorted her to his vehicle, hand in hand. He opened the door and lifted her inside, to her surprise.

He drove a suped up Jeep. She'd always loved them! It was large and comfortable with real leather seats, and an expensive sound system. It smelled clean too, like he'd just washed it. Gretchen smiled, thinking he'd probably done that for her.

This date was already starting out way better than she'd hoped. She smiled as the promise of something warm and bright began to tease her mind and heart. Warning bells should have been going off by now, but Reg was smiling at her, and Gretchen sighed wistfully.

She was not asking for rainbows, but wouldn't it be nice if this turned into something more than a meal?

*A girl can dream.*

*Sigh.*

# Chapter Ten

"Sorry, I should have rented something nicer for you," Reg began.

Gretchen shook her head, stopping his apology in its tracks. It was strange, but she wanted to reassure him. Honesty was something she tried for in all things, and whatever this turned into, she was not going to start it with silly little games most people played. She liked reg and his car and she wanted him to know it.

"No way," she began, touching his forearm lightly and watching in surprise the way the big man seemed to shudder at her touch.

*Interesting.*

"I really like Jeeps, Reg. This one is fantastic,

especially the color," she explained and ran her hands over the armrest of her warm leather seat.

The exterior was a deep, blood red that she rarely saw on this kind of vehicle, and the interior was black with that same dark red trim. It was a helluva a car and it suited him, big as he was. She could not see him driving a Prius.

"Really? Thank you. Some of the roads out here can get bad in rough weather, and I'm a big guy and I work in construction, so it helps to have something like this."

"That's right, you work for Elissa's husband," she replied and nodded at him.

"Yes, I do. I've been with Maverick Development since I was a cu-, *uh*, a kid."

Gretchen was fascinated by that line of work. She was great with scissors but couldn't do crap with a hammer or screwdriver.

"That is so cool. What do you do exactly?" she asked as he turned the corner.

"I guess, I'm a jack of all trades. I work in demolition, masonry, ironwork, and I'm a certified electrician as well. We have some local government contracts, and do a lot of roadwork, but we've been known to take on private projects."

"That's awesome that you can do all that. And I

had no idea Maverick Development was so big," she said, impressed by his skill set.

"You don't think I'm just some dumb contractor?" he asked lightly, but she sensed his tension.

"Of course not," she replied without hesitation. "Why? Do you think I'm just a dumb hair stylist?"

"What? No way! If I gave you that impression---" he almost shouted. The poor guy was tripping over himself apologizing, and she felt bad for teasing him.

"Reggie, relax. I was only kidding," Gretchen said and placed a hand on his arm. She liked the feel of his muscles beneath her fingers, and even better the way he glanced at her, one eyebrow raised as he maneuvered the vehicle down the street.

"Reggie?"

"Oh, sorry. I have this habit of shortening names. Do you mind?" she asked and bit her lip.

"Not at all, but you're the only one who can call me that," he replied, and winked.

A few minutes later, they pulled into the parking lot of a posh steakhouse and her eyes widened. This was a really nice place for a first date. One could say Reg was trying to impress her, and she wondered if that were true.

*Gulp.*

"Everything okay?"

"Yes, it looks great," she returned shyly.

"I am happy you like it. Hold up," he said when she reached for the handle. "Let me get that door for you, *shona*."

Gretchen cocked her head at the strange word, but she didn't mind it. She was so nervous he could've called her anything at all, and it would've been fine.

Gretchen tried to stop her body from reacting to him, but it was a losing battle. She got shivers all over just from being near his large, muscular frame.

Reg helped her out of the car, his big hand engulfing hers. He kept hold of it while they entered the establishment. After giving the hostess his name, he guided her to their table, ignoring the server's rapt expression as she looked Reg up and down in his black pants and blue button-down shirt.

Gretchen could hardly blame the woman. He was so freaking hot. She was ready to swoon just from having his hand on her elbow.

Imagine *her* swooning?

Yeah, she was definitely overdue for a little adult playtime. If the evening went well, maybe she would get to see more of Reginald Cray. A lot more.

They seemed to talk about everything, work, movies, music, food. He was funny and bright, and so damn intense with his long dark stares and the way he kept finding excuses to touch her.

She was wound so tightly, her body seemed to light up like the fourth of July from the slightest brush if his fingertips against her hand as he held a menu out to her. She wanted him, and she was woman enough to admit it to herself.

That was a first for Gretchen. Usually, it took a while for her to feel comfortable enough to consider sex with a man. But for some reason, Reg made her want to run right into his arms.

"You do eat meat, right?" he asked, interrupting her naughty thoughts as he looked over the evening's specials.

"Oh, yeah. You never have to worry about that, Reggie. As you can see, I eat everything," she motioned to her body and shrugged.

"I'm not sure I get what you mean," he said, eyes flashing at her. "If that was meant as some kind of dig about your body, I don't understand it. From where I am sitting, you look perfect," he growled, and cocked his head to the side as he nailed her with his steady blue stare.

It was meant to be a joke. Something she did to relieve any pressure from those around her to feel like they had to either avoid her fluffiness or make excuses for it. Gretchen liked food. She was a big healthy girl and made no apologies for it.

The way he continued to watch her was unsettling. What was he playing at? Surely, the man had eyes. Gretchen loved her body, but she wasn't unaware of it. She was a big girl and definitely not the standard of beauty in today's world.

"I just meant, it's obvious that I like food. I'm a big girl, and I know it," she said unapologetically.

"I know we just met," Reg began, and leaned forward, crowding her in the small booth they shared. "But I need to tell you a few things, just to set the record straight," he continued, and she saw the muscles in his neck tense as he spoke. Fuck, that was hot.

"*A*, you're a beautiful woman. So beautiful, I can't stop thinking about you. Your sky blue eyes, those pink pouty lips, and those crazy sexy highlights in your hair. *B*, you are the perfect size. Every dip and curve of your body is a fucking work of art. I have not been able to get it out of my head all day, and I tried, *shona*, but it was no good."

"You did?"

"Yeah, I did. But I can't stop thinking about you. I want to get you alone so bad I can taste it. I want to explore every single inch of that delectable body of yours. I want to kiss, lick, and touch every inch of you until you are screaming with pleasure. Wait a second, please," he raised a hand, halting her speech before she could comment.

"Don't think I have any intentions of taking advantage of you, or that I expect to be paid for a meal in that way. You are in control here, and I will do anything you want. I mean *anything, shona*" he continued in a voice so low, it sent tendrils of need straight through her body.

"And *C*," he said, still not finished. "You should know, this is not just about sex. I'm head over heels absolutely crazy about you. I know it is fast, but that's how I am built. I promise, Gretchen, if you let me, I'm going to prove myself to you before this night is over," he stated bluntly.

Gretchen swallowed.

*Holy shit.*

"Now, how do you like your steak?" he asked, glancing back over the menu as if he hadn't just said things that left her sitting there in a puddle of her own need.

"Uh, rare to medium rare."

"Good enough," he said, nodding and signaling for the waitress.

No one had ever said anything like that to

Gretchen before. She watched him, frowning a little as he continued to glance over the selections. What was she supposed to do with this information? With the knowledge that this stunning specimen of man had just confessed to wanting her.

She closed her eyes for a second and took a fortifying breath. A levelheaded woman most of the time, she'd never been one to rush into things, but Gretchen already knew where this night was headed. She couldn't wait. Wanting him was as natural as breathing, and she did, so very much.

He ordered a bunch of appetizers which they shared, then went for king-sized cuts of rare prime rib with au jus. He added creamed spinach and potatoes au gratin on the side, looking at her for confirmation. She simply nodded.

"This way we can share everything, if you like," he said, and she just nodded in agreement.

Gretchen loved sharing food, but she was still reeling from his little speech. The man had rendered her mute with that lengthy confession.

"Did I make you uncomfortable? I am so sorry, I'm not the best speaker in the world," he started, but she shook her head.

"It's not that, it's just no one ever said those things to me before."

"Good," he told her. "I'd hate to have to start a kill list on our first date," he said teasing her some more.

"Yeah, that's second date stuff."

After that, she felt relieved. Reg was surprisingly easy to talk to and she shared some of the day's goings ons.

"I am so proud of you," he said, and she felt her cheeks heat. "I am sorry if that sounds strange, but I can't help it. You are one fierce woman, Gretchen Kaepernick. I mean moving and starting a business in the same week? Holy hell, *shona*, you blow me away."

"Thank you," she murmured, ridiculously pleased by his praise.

The food started to arrive, and their conversation lapsed as they ate, and *oohed* and *aaaahed* over the dishes. The shrimp cocktail and raw oysters were superb. By the time their entrees arrived, she was almost too full to eat.

Reg solved that problem by placing his fork at her mouth. He fed her a bite of this and that, and before she knew it, she'd tried everything.

At first, Gretchen chewed her food slowly and thoroughly, scared to death she was going to choke from her nerves alone. As the night progressed, she felt her anxiety lessen. Reg was gorgeous, but he was levelheaded and down to earth.

They talked about every subject from politics, and religion, to mundane chatter about reality TV and what books they liked to read. It seemed he preferred fiction, mainly horror, while she enjoyed biographies and the occasional gooey romance.

"You know, you've got a lot more to you than meets the eye, Reginald Cray."

"Reginald? What happened to Reggie?"

"Reggie," she replied, and scrunched her nose playfully.

After his very forward and panty-melting confession, she had to admit to having a little bit of trouble concentrating. Her senses were going haywire. Whenever he laughed at something she said, and each time she caught him staring at her, Gretchen's pulse sped up like crazy.

After the waitress took their dishes, she came back with coffee and dessert. Gretchen shook her head. Really, she was so full, but Reg fed her a forkful of chocolate cheesecake dripping caramel sauce from his plate. Gretchen moaned in pleasure at the sinfully sweet taste.

"Wow, you look gorgeous when you eat cheesecake, *shona*," he murmured.

"That's a ridiculous thing to say," she replied, opening her mouth for another bite.

Gretchen purposefully used her tongue to lick the fork clean and the smoldering look he gave her was reward enough for that. Reg moved closer to her, his big body touching hers, one arm around her back as he fed her another, then a third bite. She lifted her fork, giving him a taste, but he declined.

"I'd rather taste it from your lips," he said, leaning down and brushing his mouth against hers.

Gretchen swooned then. Like really swooned. Reg's big body pressed against hers as he groaned into her mouth. His lips, impossibly soft, moved against hers, until she moaned, giving him the opening he needed.

Then his tongue was there, pressing into her mouth, tasting every inch of the hot wet cavern, until Gretchen thought she was going to come from just a kiss alone. It was enough to make her panties damp and her pulse race.

*Holy fuck.*

There was no going back. She wanted him. Hell, more than that.

Gretchen was desperate to have him.

He stopped their kiss, breathing like an Olympian. His eyes were closed, but she was completely amazed by his passionate display. Thank goodness they were in a secluded corner. She wasn't much for being gawked at, and who could help but stare when a man that looked that good was all but fucking her in public.

It was only a kiss, but it felt like so much more. Gretchen was on fire, and there was only one thing that could sate her impassioned need.

*Him.*

"Let's get out of here," he said, and took her hand.

Reg dropped a couple of bills on the table and took her outside.

Before he opened it, Reg backed her up against the door of his blood red Jeep, careful to mind the handle didn't dig into her. She loved how thoughtful he was, and even more, how much he seemed to want her. Gretchen moaned as he pressed his hard body into hers, claiming her mouth again in an all-consuming kiss.

Damn, he felt good. So big and hard and hot. She was ready to jump him right there.

"It might kill me, *shona*, but please, I am begging you, if you don't want me to finish this tonight tell me to stop. Tell me no. I will take you home and drive away, sweet Gretchen, but only if you tell me to," he growled.

She took a moment to think about what he was saying, then opening her eyes and gazing up at his, Gretchen replied with the only thing she could say.

"Yes."

"okay, I'll take you home and---"

"No," she said, grinning. "I am saying *yes*, Reg. I want this. I want you," she said, and it was the truth.

She was more than ready for him to do what his eyes promised. More than ready to drop all pretenses and do what it was her body was telling her too.

"Gretchen," he said her name in a low, gravelly voice that had her entire body going taut with need.

He placed his hands on either side of her face slowly, carefully, giving her ample time to refuse him. But Gretchen wasn't stupid or crazy.

There was no way in Hell she was walking away from Reg. he leaned forward until all she could see was him.

Larger than life, sexy as sin, the man smelled like chocolate and spice. His hot body was crushing hers, but still, his arms were protecting her from the Jeep's door. Every inch of him was hot and hard and so fucking sexy.

"Kissing you is addictive, *shona,* just like I knew it would be."

"It is?"

"Fuck yeah, and I have been dying to do this, ever since I laid eyes on you this morning, standing on that ladder," he growled before he dipped his head one more time, and claimed her mouth in a kiss so hot she almost melted.

Gretchen had no choice but to wrap her arms around his neck. Purely for support. At least that was what she told herself, but the truth was, she wanted to rub her body all over him.

She opened for him, an immediate response to his invasion. His flavors burst along her senses as their tongues met and tangled. Desire exploded through her veins.

Everything about Reg was exciting and intense. His strength called to her, made her crazy with need as she felt his muscles flex beneath her searching fingers. She wanted him to touch her, dammit, but his hands remained still, much to her disappointment.

"Reggie," she moaned when he broke the kiss and pressed his head against hers.

He opened his eyes, and once more, she could've sworn they glowed unnaturally in the dark parking lot. Then he was leaning back, stepping away from her, and she shivered, missing his heat immediately.

Blinking she realized another couple had exited the restaurant and were heading to their car near to where the Jeep was parked. He shielded her with his body, blocking her from their view.

*Shit.*

She wouldn't have stopped if he hadn't. His thoughtfulness warmed her.

"We have to stop, or I swear, I'll take you right here."

She nodded her understanding, and pleasure filled her. He was as out of control as she was.

*Good.* She wanted him that way. Liked knowing she could throw the big sexy man off kilter too.

Gretchen could see it on his face, his need and lust, and something more. Something wild and untamed. Maybe tonight didn't have to end with dinner and a promise to call her another night.

Maybe she could have her cake and eat it too.

"Take me home, Reggie."

# Chapter Eleven

Reg closed his eyes and thanked the gods for her. His sweet, sexy little mate was beyond even his wildest imagination. Her softly whispered plea had almost sent him to the floor with a wave of need.

*"Take me home, Reggie."*

His Tiger snapped his jaws, snarling and growling. The beast demanding he claim his mate.

Reg must have broken half a dozen traffic rules driving back to her apartment. He didn't even recall getting out of the Jeep or walking up the stairs to her apartment. The second the door closed behind them, Reg swept Gretchen up in his arms and slammed his mouth to hers.

His Tiger was snarling like crazy, his impatience

making him one ornery fuck. Reg's cock hardened painfully, but he could deal with it. She was so fucking beautiful. So lush and soft. The beast was just as anxious to sink into his mate as he was.

"You are so gorgeous," he growled, and set her down on her feet.

His hands roamed over her back and waist, her hips, and thighs. Kissing her was his new favorite pastime, he decided as he tipped her head back and plunged greedily into her mouth.

"Bed. Now," she gasped as his hands found the sweet plump globes of her ass.

In a whir of motion, he walked her backwards, never letting go of her mouth as they tugged on buttons and zippers until she was standing there in nothing but a couple of sexy scraps of silk, and a pair of fuck-me pumps. She was the most beautiful thing he'd ever seen.

Gretchen moaned, and shivers raced through him. That sound. Fuck, that fucking sound was so hoarse, so hot and needy. He loved it.

Her body was a fucking vision wrapped up like a present in dark blue material so fine, it was sheer. The fabric barely covered her cropped curls and hard-tipped breasts. He was more than grateful to whoever designed that heavenly confection, though he'd probably have to buy her several more sets, since he doubted this one would survive the night.

She had so many sexy little secrets about her. With every layer of clothing discarded, Reg unveiled something new. Little flower, stars, and heart tattoos decorated her feet, and wrists, and one fucking gorgeous work was inked across her hip and back.

The second he'd spotted the tiger blossom tree with the full image of a large Bengal tiger beneath it, his beast had roared with approval.

*Mine.*

His animal pushed the thought at him, and he wholeheartedly agreed. His mate was absolutely fucking perfect for him. And she was his. All his. Forever his. Even if she did not know it.

"Do you like it?" she asked, and bit her lip worriedly.

"It's beautiful, *shona*. Just like you," he traced the image with his fingertips lightly teasing her sensitive skin.

She was so goddamn attractive? Didn't she know? He wondered as she bit her lip. Desperate to bury himself inside her, he prolonged the foreplay. Kissing lightly, caressing her with searching, probing fingers. Reg groaned as she shivered in response.

His dick throbbed painfully in his boxer briefs.

He was dying for her touch, but the sweet woman had yet to do any exploration of her own. That was okay. All things took time, he told himself.

As if she knew what he wanted, the sweet seductress that was his mate suddenly ran her small hands along the tight muscles of his abdomen before smoothing over the hard length of his cock over his cotton briefs. She teased and squeezed, dragging a low groan from his lips.

Did the woman want to drive him out of his mind?

Finally, one bold hand dipped inside his underwear while the other wrapped around his neck. She lifted her face and mashed her mouth to his lips.

*Fuck*, her taste exploded on his tongue.

Gretchen's kiss was like dynamite. She skillfully dipped her honey sweet appendage into his mouth again and wrestled with his. One hand stroking his cock, the other tugging his hair. Fucking hell, the woman had gone and switched things before he even knew what happened. She'd become the aggressor, and he the willing participant.

His inner Tiger growled happily, the Big Cat loving the fact she was petting him and taking charge. Reg could not deny he was really fucking liking this side of her as well, but he was about to explode. And that was not gonna happen until she was coming all over him, preferably on his cock or his face. Either would work.

Need coursed through him like wildfire. Passion consumed his every thought until he didn't know where to start. He growled deep in his chest, the rumbling sound seemed to make her kisses slow.

"Touch me," she commanded, and just like that, he went into action.

He took her hands and wrested them over her head as he pushed her back onto the mattress.

"The shoes stay," he growled, and took her nod as a yes.

Finally, he had his mate beneath him, and Reg was going to show her exactly what he could offer. Pleasure like no one else could give, and him, all of him if she wanted.

*Please want me*, he silently begged.

"Keep your hands here. Don't move or I'll stop."

Her eyes snapped to his, angry and tempted to test him at first. She lowered her hands, and his withdrew from her body, then she returned to the headboard, and he grinned. He knew he had her. Reg saw the moment she decided to go with it.

*Thank fuck.*

He was taking a gamble, and he knew it, but the

fact was if she kept stroking his cock the way she was, he was going to come before he even got her completely naked.

This way, he got back some control, and with a little luck, she'd love what he was going to do.

"That's good, *shona*. Now, don't move, I would hate to stop before I make you scream," he growled, and sucked her bottom lip into his mouth.

His teeth scraped the plump flesh. Teasing it with his tongue until suddenly, he bit down, but he didn't dare break skin. Not yet. The move was meant to arouse, not to hurt or claim. Judging from the scent coming off her, she more than liked it, and so he continued.

Leaving her hands above her head, Reg released his grip on them and used his fingers to trace the slope of her neck, down the curve of her clavicle, to her beautiful silk-covered breasts. Growling deep in his chest, Reg tugged the material causing one plump nipple to pop out. Like a fresh picked berry, pink and ripe. It beckoned him and the Tiger inside him roared.

"Mine," he growled the word and sucked the sweet nub into his mouth.

Gretchen moaned and writhed beneath him as he fondled her sweet flesh, freeing both of her perfect mounds from the confines of the sexy as hell bra. He laved attention on one plump breast then the other. Suckling and nibbling on her soft skin while he tore the bra from her body.

Once he was satisfied, he'd shown his appreciation for her wonderful bosoms, Reg travelled lower. He sank his tongue into her bellybutton in a hot, wet kiss before sliding down her legs. He parted them, taking her wonderfully thick thighs in both his hands and pressing down.

Reg growled deeply as her light floral scent mixed with the headier fragrance of her arousal wrapped around him and took root. His cock hardened even more, threatening to punch a hole through his briefs.

"Reggie," she moaned his name, and his Tiger chuffed appreciatively.

She wanted him. That was good. His mate should always want him, and he should always deliver.

"I love your legs, *shona*. Wanna taste them, here and here," he told her, dropping soft kisses along her thighs, all the way to the sweet spots beneath her knees, to her calves, and finally to her delicate ankles.

Her feet were still inside her *fuck me pumps* and he intended to keep them there. Reg raised both her legs until her heels were on the mattress, pushing them apart so her sex was on glorious display. Reg knelt and looked at the succulent image she made.

Knees bent, legs splayed, pussy dripping through her sheer panties, his *shona* was a fucking work of art. Gretchen's back arched and she gasped, anticipation making it all that much sweeter.

He used his hands and lips to trace the slope of her long legs until his fingertips swept over her hips and ass, to her crack. He teased and toyed with his fingers, moving back towards her front. Inch by inch, until he traced her trembling lips, guiding over her slit through the thin blue fabric that only barely shielded her from him.

The swatch of blue silk did nothing to hide her cropped curls from his piercing gaze, or her delicious scent from his nostrils. Reg salivated, actually fucking drooled, that was how desperate he was to get a taste.

"Reggie," she moaned his name again as his fingers traced around the edge of her panties.

"What is it, *shona*? What do you need?"

Reg moved his big shoulders between those succulent thighs of hers, forcing them to open wider to make room for him. He leaned forward, blowing a hot breath on the damp material. The scent of her had his fangs begging to be loosed, but he held onto his control.

*Barely.*

"Need you."

"So pretty, *shona*. But I need you to be specific," he growled.

"Touch me. Kiss me. Please, Reg," she begged.

"So sweet, my *shona*. Gonna kiss you, and touch you, and lick this pretty pussy until you scream for me, baby," he growled the words and kissed her through the blue fabric.

"Yes, oh yes," she moaned, and reached down with her hands.

"Ah, ah, ah," he chided. "Keep those hands up," he stopped his ministrations, and she whimpered, but she listened, raising her arms immediately.

"No fair, I want to touch too."

"Not yet, *shona*. I want this to last. If you start touching me, it'll be over way too soon," he said, wanting her to understand.

"Okay," she nodded, wiggling her hips on the comforter suggestively. She was driving his beast insane sweet little vixen that she was, and she didn't even know it.

*Mine.*

"Good. Keep them up there like a good girl, and

I'll give you what you want," he growled, pulling her panties to the side, revealing her moist lips.

The flowery scent of her was stronger with her need.

*Fucking delicious*, he thought as his tongue parted her slick folds with one long swipe.

"Holy shit," she yelled, back arching as he did it again, and again.

Heaven. Gretchen tasted like goddamn heaven. She was the sweetest cream he'd ever had. And he wanted more.

Reg pushed her legs farther apart and continued to suckle her plump sex. She moaned and writhed, but smart girl, she did not move her hands again other than to grip the comforter. Good, because he wasn't finished yet.

Bucking her hips against his mouth, Reg lapped at her like the animal he was, like a good kitty, he took his time. His strokes long and slow.

*Steady does it* was his motto. Yeah, he could not wait to pound home into her sweet little pussy, but he wasn't quite done with his cream yet. He took ahold of her sweet ass cheeks, lifting her so he could better feast on her *purrfectly* plump pussy.

Reg's chest rumbled with his beast as he licked at her cream, swallowing down every last drop.

"Oh my god, Reggie," she was panting now, and he knew she was close.

She had the most amazing flavor. Made especially by the universe and all just for him. He wanted to eat all of her, to devour her whole. But first, he had to make her come.

"Like this *shona*, want more?"

"Oh god. Yes. More," she begged, and he knew right then he would do anything for her.

"I need you to come for me, then you can have anything you want," he growled, and slipped two thick digits into her channel, stretching the tight passage, and massaging her core. He almost went cross-eyed when her channel squeezed, and fuck, he couldn't wait to see how good she was going to feel on his cock.

"Reggie!"

"Fuck, you're tight baby. So hot and wet. Can't wait to feel you on my cock," he growled, and found her clit with his tongue. He flicked the flat side over the tiny nub, faster and harder while she moaned his name and lifted her pussy in time with his ministrations. Like an offering, he thought and growled as he fucked her with his fingers and his mouth.

This time when she reached down and grabbed onto his hair, he let her. Fuck, he hardly noticed. Her delicious little pussy squeezed his fingers tighter, and his dick throbbed in response.

"Come on, *shona*. Do it now, come for me," he growled, and closed his mouth over her clit, suckling the greedy little nub until she was bucking against him and crying out wildly.

Reg growled, the vibration rumbling through his chest straight to her sex. He scraped that little nubbin with one long fang and that was when his mate completely fell apart with his name on her lips.

"*OHFUCKOHGOD!*"

"Mine," he snarled the word, and rose to his knees.

Ripping her panties with one hard tug, he took his cock in his hands and pushed into her. Slowly, deliberately, his eyes watching her every reaction as he finally sunk home.

"Mine!" Reg roared aloud, staking his claim with his body and words. The rightness of it all echoed through to his soul.

Gretchen's eyes met his, lust glazed even on the heels of her release. She reached for him, scratching her nails down his back, and grabbing onto his hips as he began to plunge deeper into her slick heat.

The connection between them seemed to pulse

and throb like a living thing. One that wouldn't be denied.

"Yes," she said, as if answering him, and the Tiger in him went wild.

*Mate.*

<h1 style="text-align:center">Chapter Twelve</h1>

Gretchen cried aloud as Reggie filled her with his magnificent cock. The man was big. Bigger than big. He was so fucking huge, she thought he'd split her in two.

"I don't think I can," she moaned worried, as he tilted her hips, sinking even deeper.

"Yes, you can, *shona*. You were made for me," he grunted, so sure and careful as he waited for her body to adjust.

He was whispering to her, sweet little terms of endearment and words of praise. Gretchen relaxed around him. Slowly, the burn of his invasion lessened. It became hot and more intensely pleasurable than anything else she'd ever felt.

Like her pussy had a brain of its own, and suddenly, it was all about welcoming all the very man inches of his impossibly thick, steel hard length. She'd never been so full. Reg was stretching her tight channel to the max, brushing every inch of her passage with his girthy, veined member.

"Oh god, Reggie," she moaned and could hardly catch her breath.

Cream dripped from her pussy, coating him, she knew, and dripping down her thighs. Her own body was working to make his passage slick and smooth for when he finally got to moving. Which, with any luck, would be any second now.

"You feel like pure heaven, *shona*," he growled, and yes, she meant growled, like some kind of beast.

Then he dipped his head and claimed her mouth surely as his cock was claiming her body. Reg's whole body shuddered, and her heart swelled, knowing this meant something to the big man. He kissed her like he was desperate for her, and Gretchen opened for him, tasting her sex on his lips.

Fucking hell. She hadn't expected that to turn her on, but it was raw, and it was hot, and it was him. Wild, powerful, heady, and sexy as hell. The way she wanted it. The way she wanted him.

"Want you. Want to make you mine. You want that, *shona*? Want to be mine? Forever," his deep blue eyes flashed in the darkness of the room and her whole body lit up in response.

Gretchen nodded her head, incapable of speech. Yes. Sounded good to her. She could be his tonight.

Hell, she already was.

Reg began thrusting his hips. His wonderful cock was moving inside of her now, like he was born to make love to her. Touching places no one had ever reached, Reggie fucked her like a goddamn champ.

*Push in, pull out, slam, withdraw, and repeat.*

Gretchen couldn't speak, hell, she could hardly think. Every cell in her body was attuned to him and the magical things he was doing to her. Electricity sizzled along her skin, blood raced through her veins, and her heart thundered inside of her. She felt like a volcano. Passion bubbled beneath the surface, ready to explode out of her any moment now.

She wrapped her legs around his waist. Loving the feel of his rock hard abs against her thighs. He had scrolling ink tattoos across his chest and arms. Beautiful tribal tatts that she'd enjoy tracing with her hands later, and if she were lucky, her tongue.

She kicked off her shoes, ignoring the heavy thud as they landed on the floor, so that she could dig her heels into his firm backside. She pressed them against him, urging him on as he stroked deep, so very deep, inside her.

"More," she demanded, loving the way he fucked her.

Hell, she could find herself falling over the edge with this man. That was dangerous territory, but nothing could stop the thought from racing through her mind.

Gretchen always was a little pushy, but she couldn't help it. She wanted him, all of him, and she could tell he was holding back.

"Easy," he said, but she wasn't having that.

"No, give me more, Reggie. I can take it. I want it. Give me all of you. Now."

She saw the instant he decided to let go, and all she had to do was hold on. Fingernails digging into her hips he pushed his cock deep and flipped them over so that he was in a sitting position with Gretchen astride him.

"Fuck," she moaned and shifted until she was able to find purchase.

Feet flat on the bed, she crouched over him, using her legs to pump her pussy up and down on his cock.

"That's it, baby. Now you're in control. You like

that, my wild one, don't you?"

"Reggie! Fuck," she moaned.

"Ride me, *shona*. Give me everything you've got," he groaned, gripping her ass with his large hands.

Gretchen was completely on board with this plan. It wasn't every day a man that looked like Reg was willing to be her personal sex slave. She lifted and pressed down, slowly at first, then faster and harder.

"Fuck, *shona*. That's it! You're so fucking good at that, baby. So hot and wet and tight. Take me, go on, take all of me," he growled, thrusting upwards to meet her every descent.

Gretchen ground her pussy against his pubis with each and every slide of her slick sex. She increased speed, faster and harder, until she seemed closer and closer to her ultimate release.

Fingers gripping his shoulders, she scratched at him just to keep her grip. Reg hissed and growled as she pulsed around his invading sex. Grinding and sliding, up and down, faster, and faster, until he was just as breathless as she.

She could feel his cock pulsating deep within her, the perfect curve of it brushing against that special spot inside of her that no one had ever reached. Wetness dripped from her pussy, coating his dick, covering them both in the heady scent of sex that filled the whole room.

"Mine," he growled the word, and her pussy clenched, squeezing him tightly.

She'd never been much for possessive assholes, but that word from his lips sent tendrils of excitement racing down her spine. She didn't know why. It was too dominating, too clingy, almost Neanderthal-like, but her body seemed to really like it.

Gretchen panted as together they raced to fulfillment. Louder she groaned, eyes glued to his as she continued to ride his body.

"So fucking good," he grunted.

Gretchen rocked her body, encouraged by his praise. Back and forth, up, and down, faster still. There it was, just out of reach.

Reggie seemed to understand. He grabbed her hips and started moving her quicker, harder, slamming her down onto his cock. Again and again. Both of them grunting as she chased her orgasm until that one explosive moment when it nearly overcame her.

Gretchen cried out as her pussy convulsed around him, milking his cock, but he was not through yet. Reggie flipped them once more, impaling her with his even harder shaft.

Need, desperate and raw, filled her. She wanted him to come, Now. She'd never craved a man like this, never sought or received pleasure with such glorious abandon.

Perspiration dotted his forehead as he thrust his hips once, twice, two more times. Gretchen's pussy clenched and spasmed. Pure ecstasy shot through her. She was barely aware of him as he lowered his head and sucked her neck, biting the flesh and tipping her orgasm into astronomical proportions.

The entire world went white as blinding light filled her vision. She felt him. All of him. His warm body hovered over and around her. His thick, wonderful cock pulsed heavily as he spilled his cum into her womb. Never before had she felt something so phenomenal.

This night would change her forever, somehow, she just knew it. Nothing would ever be the same again. How could it be? She'd just been fucked silly by what was surely a god come down to earth just for her.

*Sigh.*

It was a nice daydream, but the truth was Reg

was flesh and blood just like her. Soon, he would tire of her. That was how things like this worked out for Gretchen. He would move on, and she would have to learn to cope with the loss.

*Shit.*

She didn't want to have negative thoughts like that. Especially not now when her body was still shivering with the strength of her release, and his heart still pounded against hers.

She breathed deep, sucking in that spicy masculine scent that was all Reggie. He pressed down against her, wrapping his arms around her like steel bands in a good, hard embrace.

Then he leaned down and captured her mouth in a long, deep kiss. They both moaned the loss as he slowly withdrew completely from her slick heat.

Amazing man that he was, Reg reached over to a pile of freshly laundered towels that were folded in a basket she'd left on the floor earlier that day.

He took one and used it to pat some of the stickiness from her legs, making her more comfortable before tossing it in the direction of the open bathroom.

*Fuck.*

She'd forgotten about condoms. Gretchen was on

the pill, having never had regular periods, and she had regular checkups with her doctor. Reg had mentioned something similar at dinner, not that he was on the pill, but that he had not had a lady friend in months and enjoyed regular health checkups, a necessity for his job.

She knew birth control was not 100% effective, but she would worry about that later. Right then, she could hardly form a complete thought. Tiny, little aftershocks zipped through her frame, making her shudder and tremble for several, long minutes that followed.

It took all that time and more for her breathing to even out. Her entire body still tingled, wonder and awe warred within her, each one bidding for the top spot in her emotional database, but nothing could knock out the feeling of rightness that coursed through her blood.

Shocked eyes met his smoldering ones. She thought she saw something more than satisfaction lurking in those inky blue depths. But it was too soon to make that assumption, wasn't it?

He brushed the hair from her cheek, nuzzling her face with his own while he worked to steady his own breathing. Gretchen's pulse was still racing. She had no idea what to do next. What did a girl say at a time like this, anyway?

*Hey, that was fun. My pink bits really enjoyed sexy times with you. So, uh, do you wanna do it again?*

*Shit.*

Words were inadequate. That was literally the most explosive sex of her life. Her entire body seemed to buzz and shudder with more, tiny little aftershocks from her multiple orgasms.

It was amazing. Fantastic. Really and truly. But *and it was a sad but*, it was just sex. She couldn't afford to risk her heart.

Not now, when she'd just moved to a new town and started her own place of business for the first time.

It was time to say goodnight, she thought sadly, and turned to see him staring, just watching her with a guarded expression on his handsome face. Her heart thundered in her chest.

Behind that mask, his deep blue eyes were full of emotion. She wasn't exactly ready to think about what that meant just yet. True, she'd jumped right into this, right into bed, but she'd assumed it was a regular thing for him. But with the way he was looking at her, she wasn't so sure.

"That was---"

"Incredible," he supplied the word for her, but even that felt insufficient.

Her cheeks heated up again and she could only imagine how unflattering she looked all pink and blotchy.

"So beautiful, *shona*," he said, and shifted so that he was lying on his side with an arm wrapped around her middle.

Suddenly self-conscious, she grabbed a sheet and tugged it over her. He mistook it to mean she was cold and proceeded to cover her naked flesh with the comforter. The gesture warmed her like no blanket ever could.

"Better?"

"Yes, thanks," she replied, and felt her face blush even harder.

Gretchen felt as if she were on fire, she bit her lip anxiously. Unsure of what came next, she avoided his eyes until he turned her face with a gentle finger on her chin.

"Gretchen, there's something I have to tell you."

"Okay," she waited expectantly.

"I don't know where to start," Reg began and blinked a few times as if gathering his thoughts.

She noted the worry in his gaze and held her breath. Whatever it was, she didn't know if she could handle it. Especially since the last hour had basically tilted her world on its axis.

Reg had pretty much ruined her for any other man in the world. Shit. How was she supposed to recover? Her chest tightened and she could hardly breathe.

She felt trapped

"I, that is you, you are a very special woman---"

Her stomach squeezed inside her body, she had to sit up. She knew what was coming, what he was trying to say, but *geez*, couldn't he have just given her a kiss and left? Talk about tactless.

"Look, Reggie, I understand really. You can lock the bottom lock on your way out. I'm gonna jump in the shower. I have an early day tomorrow."

She scuttled out of bed with the sheet around her body and made for the bathroom.

"Wait a second!" Reg called out and had the nerve to sound angry as he leapt out of the bed and followed her.

He stopped her progression by pinning her against the wall. Gretchen growled at him, while her body heated, and heartbeat raced.

*Traitorous thing!*

She didn't know whether to be angry or turned

on. But she hated confrontations, and just wanted to get it over with.

"Look, I'm a physical kind of guy. I don't have a way with words, so maybe I chose the wrong ones, but please do not walk away from me. I could not stand it," he said, and his eyes pleaded with her.

"What?" she asked. Embarrassment reared its ugly head and Gretchen could hardly meet his eyes.

"I don't know what you think I was trying to say, but it wasn't goodbye, Gretch."

"Fine. Well, what are you trying to say then? You had a nice time, and now you have to go? I mean, I get it---"

"No, that is not it at all," he roared. "I am trying to tell you that you're my mate, but you're running off before I even have the chance!"

Gretchen stared at him, her confusion written all over her. Why did he look like she just kicked his puppy? And what the fuck was a mate?

"Mate? What the heck are you talking about?"

He moved back a step and ran a hand through his newly shorn locks. She had to admit she'd done a great job with his hair. He looked damn good. Still, that did not mean she had to put up with crazy.

Gretchen supposed she should just thank him for

that rock hard body she'd thoroughly enjoyed just moments ago. Then wipe her hands of the man.

Watching his fine physique as he paced in front of her, she felt familiar tingles begin in her belly and lower. He stopped pacing, nostrils flaring animalistically, he turned his head, capturing her in his steel gaze.

"Dammit woman, I can barely get through this without wanting to throw you down on that bed and having you all over again, but it is important for me to say. I need you to understand, so cut it out, okay?"

She swallowed hard. Her pussy ached and wetness slid down her legs in preparation for him. Only him. She gritted her teeth and stared at him pointedly.

*Dammit,* she was turning into some kind of slut for the guy, and she hardly knew him.

"You don't owe me anything. I am a big girl, Reg. Just say what you have to say," she said, hating the insecurities that rose within her.

"I am not like other guys," he started.

"No shit," she rolled her eyes. Of course he wasn't. She just had to look at him to know that, for fuck's sake.

"No, look, I mean, I'm not human."

"What?"

"Gretch, I'm a *Shifter*, a Tiger to be exact. And you are my mate."

Gretchen felt her body grow cold as she saw the expectant look on Reg's face. Too many emotions to name rose like the tide, the foremost being humiliation.

Did he think she was some kind of desperate idiot? Had he seen her romance novels on the shelf, and thought this would be a fun way to tease her? What a dick!

"I, uh, I think you have to leave now."

"Gretchen, look I swear-"

"I said leave, Reggie. Now."

She watched the blood drain from his face as he grabbed his pants and tugged them on. He didn't bother with his underwear or his shirt. Just picked up his shoes as he walked to the door.

"Please, *shona*. Let me explain. Your my mate. That bite I gave you is important, I got so excited when you said yes, and my beast---"

"I think you've said enough. I want you to leave my apartment. Now."

"Gretchen, I am not lying to you---"

"No, you're making fun of me, and that is unacceptable."

"What? I am not. Please, just let me show you---"

"Reg, leave before I call the cops."

"Fuck. I'm sorry, I did this wrong, Gretchen, but---"

She had already pushed him out, walking him backwards to the door. Gretchen slammed it and threw the locks. Angry at herself and ignoring his knocks.

"I'll go because you want me to, but we are not finished, *shona*," he said through the closed door, but she was already walking away.

Emptiness threatened to consume her as she washed away the evidence of the night's activities from her skin. Tears streamed down her face as she ripped the still warm sheets from her bed and tossed everything into the washing machine. She wanted no reminders of her stupidity.

Gretchen had heard some strange things before, but never had she had to deal with anything like this. The man was a lunatic. Or he was mean, picking up on her love of supernatural romance novels to poke fun of her.

Or even worse, he was both. Crazy and mean. She wouldn't tell Elissa. One, because she didn't want to upset her pregnant friend. And two, she did not want to get him fired.

Whatever his delusion, he wasn't a bad guy. Just crazy.

Gretchen would do well enough to just forget about Reginald Cray. At least that's what she told herself while she tossed and turned that night.

*Focus on Cut It Out, and cut all the bullshit out of your life, literally.*

*You can do it.*

# Chapter Thirteen

Gretchen heaved a sigh as she swept up hair and dirt from the day off the tiled floor of *Cut It Out*. The last few days had been rough on her, physically and emotionally. Who knew running a business could be so taxing?

*Oh hell.*

Who was she kidding? That wasn't the cause of all her worries, and she knew it. She was missing Reg something fierce. Odd, considering their whole relationship, if she could even call it that, had lasted just one day.

She'd just never been so thoroughly and completely captivated by a man. He was on her mind every second of the day. His smile, his laugh, his sexy as fuck body.

But even when she forced herself to stop thinking about him, there was another horrifying fact. Gretchen had felt physically sick ever since he left that night.

Not just her heart, which felt as if she'd split it in two, but everything else. Even her hair hurt.

She had the worst stomach cramps ever. Maybe it was something she ate? Her period wasn't do for another few days, and she doubted her one-night stand with Mr. Sexy-Crazy-Pants had made her pregnant. A home test confirmed she was not knocked-up. Thank goodness. But for some reason, the thought made her sad.

*OMFG. Now, you sound crazy*, she thought to herself.

"Okay, boss lady. I am done! You have a good one, *chica*," Marion called out.

He interrupted her train of thought and waved as he took off for the evening. He'd followed Bonnie by just minutes, and now, she was truly alone in the salon.

Gretchen smiled and waved goodbye. She was so happy she had found the two of them. They were hard workers, friendly and easygoing too, which was a huge plus in her world.

The other new girl, April, was a bit quiet, but she

did good work. After supervising her for her first few cuts, Gretchen approved and offered her a position. The young woman immediately accepted. It was another win-win. Unfortunately, Gretchen didn't feel like she'd won anything.

It had been three days since she'd last seen Reg. Three days since he'd wined, dined, then proceeded to fuck her stupid. She'd been uncertain, and a little worried about what would happen afterwards. She'd always hated awkward mornings after, but they didn't even get that far.

He'd made her feel so special, and just, well, *good*, with his over the top attentions, and the amazing way he seemed attuned to her every want and need. But those things had never lasted for Gretchen before, and this was shorter than any other past dating fail. She was sadly lacking romantically speaking.

Maybe it was a blessing in disguise. Maybe she'd saved her heart from taking a huge blow by cutting things short.

Nothing could have really prepared her for the bomb he'd dropped on her. Nor for the consequential kicking him out of her apartment that occurred only minutes later.

Ever since that night, Gretchen had been dodging

his calls and messages. She'd even locked herself in the bathroom the two times he'd come to the salon to try and talk to her.

At least he had enough couth not to cause a scene at her place of business. She'd even been dodging Elissa's calls in order to avoid having to talk about Reg.

She shook her head and wiped the stray tear that rolled down her face. Did he really think she was going to believe him?

A Shifter? And not just any Shifter, but her favorite animal. A Tiger. Really?

The man was playing on the fact she'd told him about her affinity for the majestic creatures, and he must have seen her bookshelves to boot. A simple google search would have told him what any of the titles were about.

But really? Claiming to be A Shifter after taking her to bed was beyond a joke. Maybe that part was not true. Maybe the guy was just plain old-fashioned crazy.

The bells above the salon door sounded, and she turned to see her shop being invaded by none other than Elissa, Jessica, and Kylie. Shoulders slumped, she turned to the women, and waved half-heartedly.

Pretending to be happy would have taken too much energy, and her stomach still hurt.

"Hello, ladies. Was there a get-together tonight that I forgot?"

"I'm gonna pretend you didn't just say that, young lady," Elissa scolded and paused with her hands on her belly.

Her bestie exhaled then walked over and wrapped Gretchen up in a big hug. Dang it, now she was gonna cry. Gretchen bit her lip, and hugged her friend back, careful not to smush the little ones.

"I know what you really meant to say was, thank you, beautiful Elissa for coming by to check up on me, even though I've been acting like a bitchy heifer, refusing your phone calls, and not returning your texts! You broke our *snapagram* streak, Gretch! That is a blockable offense," Elissa glared at her, and Gretchen covered her mouth to hold in a laugh.

They'd had a long one going too. 1298 days of texts and pictures back and forth. *Snapagram* was a popular phone app that could, unfortunately, cost many a job since it was a rabbit hole you could not easily crawl out of. Sigh. But it was still fun.

"Okay, okay, I'm sorry," Gretchen apologized. "Of course, I love you Elissa, and I am glad you came over to cheer me up. I am glad you all came, really, but where is Hunter?" Gretchen asked while placating her temporarily emotionally unstable friend.

She'd read somewhere that pregnancy did that to people. Something about the ups and downs caused by the hormones needed to grow a perfect tiny little human. Unfortunately, that turned usually normal people into homicidal maniacs who alternately craved ridiculous amounts of carbs while binge watching sad as fuck TV series.

Elissa had watched the *Thorn Birds* saga six times already according to Jess. That was not good for anyone's emotional health. So, no, Gretchen wasn't taking any chances with her friend. She would placate her whenever necessary.

"Oh, I left him at the house. But look, I invited someone here that I think you should finally meet," Elissa said while Gretchen greeted the other two women.

The bells jingled once more over her door and Gretchen turned to see an older man walk in. He looked friendly and stylish with a thick mane of white hair and a matching beard and mustache. Very elegant and sophisticated, and yet, he exuded a platonic warmth she had never felt. The man walked into *Cut It Out*, looking around first with a smile in his sparkling blue eyes before he turned to them.

"Am I late?"

"Not at all!"

Gretchen watched curiously as Elissa smiled and walked to the man, giving him a hug and kiss on his cheek. Elissa's eyes were wide with pleasure as she chatted with the man with the electric gaze.

*Wow.* There must be something in the air Maverick Point. Everyone had the most fascinating color eyes. Elissa turned her head again and smiled at the younger man standing just behind the strange older one. He was holding a large box filled with containers of what smelled like Chinese food.

If that was true, the two gentlemen were about to be Gretchen's new best friends. She hadn't been able to eat all day, and she was suddenly starving. Her stomach growled and she covered her mouth in embarrassment.

"Excuse me," she said to no one in particular.

"Thank you for coming. Gretchen, come over here and meet Uncle Uzzi," Elissa said, and waddled over to tug Gretchen by the hand.

"Where can I put this?" the other man asked.

"Hello, Hank. Um, right there," Elissa smiled, and gestured for him to drop the box on the coffee table that Gretchen had just wiped clean. "I think that should be fine."

"Hello Hank, um, Uncle Uzzi. I'm Gretchen Kaepernick and yes, that would be perfect, thank you so much." Gretchen smiled and shook hands, gesturing to the table.

Hank, dressed in a driver's uniform, nodded, and began unpacking the goods before he stepped back outside and returned to the stretched limo waiting outside.

"Don't mind, Hank. He always drives for me when I am out this way, but he prefers to stay with the car. Big reader, you know," Uncle Uzzi explained and walked over to look Gretchen over.

"Now, my dear, I am Uncle Uzzi and you, Gretchen, sent me an email a few weeks ago. I only realized yesterday that my reply did not send, you see, I am not used to these confounded *vunderboxes*," he said, pulling his phone out of his pocket. "Anyway, since you already had your date, I wanted to check in---"

"I am sorry," Gretchen said, not bothering to hide her shock. "But what date? You never got back to me."

"Hello Uncle Uzzi," Jessica said, interrupting after returning from the restroom.

"Hello, Jessica! How is that bear of a man treating you, well I hope?"

"Brayden is a dream, thanks."

"That's good, dear. Hello Kylie, you look lovely."

"Oh, you tease! By the way, Uncle Uzzi, I have the material for your order coming in this week. I'll be able to ship it by the end of the month," Kylie added.

"Kylie that is perfect, but didn't I tell you to call me Uncle Uzzi? Anyone who makes me pajamas must be on a first name basis with me. I insist," she barked out a laugh and everyone joined in.

Apparently, *Kisses by Kylie* offered custom pajamas for men as well.

*Note to self*, Gretchen thought and laughed along with the other women.

"But back to you, Miss Gretchen, you had a date with Reg Cray a few days ago I had already talked to the man, of course, but I have a feeling that things did not go all that smoothly," he began.

Everyone sat down around the large coffee table and handed out napkins and plastic forks as the group chatted and exchanged pleasantries. They started filling their plates with Szechuan chicken, pork dumplings, vegetable lo mein, chicken fried rice, and so many more delicious dishes.

She was still trying to gather her thoughts, but

because she hadn't realized how hungry she was her stomach grumbled uncontrollably.

"Um, I think, I need to eat," she said, her mouth was watering at the sudden whiff of the spicy, garlicky deliciousness.

"Of course, dear," Uzzi said, eyes narrowing as he watched her inhale two egg rolls and a whole order of dumplings before she knew it.

"Thank you so much for bringing this, Uncle Uzzi. I guess I was starving," Gretchen said by way of apology.

"OMG! These spring rolls are da bomb. So Gretch, you gonna tell us what happened," Elissa asked and moaned as she took another bite.

Jessica and Kylie were eating and talking lowly, not rushing her like Elissa. But Gretchen was used to her BFF's impatience. She just shrugged it off and took a sip of iced green tea Uncle Uzzi had brought to compliment the meal.

"Oh, it's my pleasure," Uncle Uzzi said, replying to her earlier *thank you.* "So, tell me why you think I didn't reply to your email if you had your date already?" Uncle Uzzi asked while nibbling an egg roll of his own.

"Well, you didn't," Gretchen said and looked around at the amused faces of her friends.

"Actually, Gretchen, Uncle Uzzi doesn't always answer in the traditional way. Sometimes Fate decides how things play out," Jessica said, hinting something she could not quite comprehend.

"What the heck are any of you talking about?"

Embarrassment, hope, sadness, and curiosity all warred within her. How was Gretchen supposed to tell them about Reg? She supposed she should confirm what they were talking about before she worried for nothing.

*Take it one step at a time, Gretchen.*

# Chapter Fourteen

She paused, waiting for her pals to fill her in. After all, no sense borrowing trouble. Uncle Uzzi turned his electric blue gaze on her.

"I am talking about Reginald Cray, dear. Didn't he take you out a few days ago?"

The old man waited for her to respond, but all she could do was blink. Shit. What could she say?

*Well, the dinner was good, the sex was better, but he turned out to be a crazy mofo, after all?*

"Oh," Gretchen said after a moment. She couldn't hide her shock or her sorrow. "I am sorry, Uncle Uzzi, but that didn't exactly pan out. Maybe there is someone else in your client list for me."

"What?" Jessica gasped.

"No way," Kylie whispered.

"Honey, what happened?" Elissa asked.

"Shhh, ladies. I am not infallible. Now, Gretchen, if you do not mind telling us, what happened?"

"Excuse me?"

She was not sure how to respond. She didn't want to hurt his reputation with the people of Maverick Point. He lived and worked there, for fuck's sake. Her bleeding heart was going to be the death of her, she thought, closing her eyes on a new wave of cramping.

"Well? What happened? He took you to dinner. Did he chew with his mouth open? Fart at the table? Make you pay?" Uncle Uzzi asked.

"No! Of course not," she said, and snorted at the very idea. "Reg has impeccable table manners, and he would never have asked me to pay the bill."

"I see. So, was he bad in bed? To, *uh*, insufficient to fill the position?" the old man pressed.

"What?" Gretchen couldn't believe how outspoken Uncle Uzzi was.

It was different and refreshing, if a little strange, but still. Should she talk about her bedroom activities with Reg with a stranger? She'd always imagined herself as a little forward, but the older man positively blew her away for sheer pluck alone.

It's not that she was keeping secrets, but how

could she tell them all the truth? That Reg was delu-sional. A madman. A nutjob.

"Come on, you're among friends," Uncle Uzzi coaxed with an open and friendly smile.

"I know he took you out to dinner, but maybe he forgot to make *you* dessert."

"Oh, uh, that is not---" Gretchen hesitated.

"I don't know about you younger people, but that was always a definite deal-breaker with my liebling. She would always emphasize the importance of a good, solid sexual relationship between lovers. She would always say, when a man has sex with a woman if he's not leaving her legs too weak to stand, then he did something wrong. So, can I assume he didn't put your needs first, if so then he will be talked to and will attend proper counseling and instructional----" Uncle Uzzi said so rapidly, it took a moment for Gretchen to catch up. It sounded as if the man was making a list or something.

"Wait! No! I mean there is nothing wrong with Reg's equipment or technique---"

"Then tell us what is wrong with him," Elissa begged.

"I'm sorry, I just don't think gossiping about him is right," Gretchen replied, starting to blush.

"Oooh! Did that selfish bastard make you do the

heavy lifting without a little oral reward?" Jessica asked and narrowed her eyes.

Gretchen moaned heavily. This was not going to be easy, but she supposed she better just tell them.

"Ladies, and Uncle Uzzi, please stop this. Reg was perfect. I mean the sex was fine-"

"Oh good! So, he did make you orgasm then?" Uncle Uzzi asked.

"Yes, okay! Sheesh, people, *yes*, okay? YES! Reg rocked my world. I orgasmed frequently. Are you happy, now?"

"Oh yay! I knew he couldn't be that bad," Elissa whispered.

"Get it, girl! Our Gretchen took a trip to slut-town," Jessica joked, breaking the tension. Everyone giggled, Gretchen included.

"Good for you. I'm so jealous. It's been a long, long time since I visited slut-town myself," Kylie sighed.

"Ladies, please," Elissa held up her hands to shush everyone. "I for one don't think name calling is necessary when a woman chooses to have inter-course with someone on their first date it is their choice---"

"Um, yeah, Liss, we know you feel that way

seeing as how you were banging my brother in like minutes of meeting him," snorted Jessica.

"What was that?" Elissa raised an eyebrow, and for a moment, she looked exactly like a schoolteacher about to lay down the law. But then, she ruined the whole thing by giggling.

"Okay, fine. Hell to the yeah, I did have sex with your brother as soon as we met, and let me tell you something, it was fan-fucking-tastic! Sex is important in any relationship. Who's with me?"

Elissa held up her hand for a fist-bump which Kylie obliged.

"Ew. Like TMI, Liss," Jessica said then made some faux barfing noises.

"Ladies," Uncle Uzzi interrupted, and nodded back at Gretchen.

"You can just shut up," Elissa returned to Jessica, then looked back at Uncle Uzzi and Gretchen. "I'm sorry, Uncle Uzzi. So, Gretch, you had sex with him, then what?"

Gretchen rolled her eyes. There was only one way to shut her bestie up. That was with the truth.

"Okay, yes, we had sex, but the guy is certifiable."

"How do you mean? Did he hurt you?" Uncle Uzzi sat up straighter, and Gretchen swore she saw fire in his blue depths.

"No, not at all! He was very sweet, wonderful really, but then, well---" she hedged.

"What's the problem then? Don't you like sex?"

"Yes, I like sex," she exhaled, and turned to everyone.

"Gretch?" Elissa's worried expression met hers. She knew she had to tell her best friend the truth.

"Okay, first, Elissa, I need you to promise you will not tell Hunter what I say here. Whatever is up with Reggie, he deserves to keep his job."

"Okay," Elissa snorted. "OMG! You call him Reggie?"

"*Shaddup*," Gretchen shook her head. "Okay, *Reg* and I had sex---"

"And? Just to reiterate, was he considerate? Did he fail in the orgasm department or the equipment department?" Uncle Uzzi asked.

"What? No. NO! NO! The equipment was fine, better than fine. It was great. Like this great."

Gretchen held her hands apart and got a few wolf whistles that made a new and terrifying green-eyed monster of a bitch rear its ugly head from deep inside her.

*Grrrrrrr.*

Where the hell did that come from? She'd never felt such a furious flash of jealousy. Her cramps were back, and she wondered if she should run to put a tampon on. No, she still had days before her period should arrive.

Gretchen shook it off and took a sip of tea to clear her head. A wave of nausea hit her, but she ignored it. Gretchen needed to focus on what she was saying. This was it, the heartbreaking truth about this whole incident with Reg.

"Okay, yes, so size-wise the guy is a dream. And yes, he made me orgasm. Several times," she informed them, her face flaming, but for some reason she didn't want these women thinking Reg was a slouch in any way, shape, or form.

"Good," Uncle Uzzi nodded, encouraging her to continue.

"He was very, very thorough and considerate."

Truth was he'd blown away all her other sexual experiences. Even before the carnal part of the evening, the date had been awesome. The food was good, the restaurant nice, and the company even better. He'd made her smile and laugh easily with his quick wit and humor.

Plus, Reg had listened to her. Like really listened. When had a guy ever done that? It had been a wonderful date. Talking to him was just so easy. She sighed sadly thinking about that amazing night.

Where did it go wrong? How had she missed the signs?

"Then what's the problem?" Uncle Uzzi cocked his head to the side, watching Gretchen intently.

"This is harder than I thought it would be to say out loud," she confided in the older man, who was essentially a stranger, but seemed to have no qualms about discussing all things personal. "The weirdness came afterwards. You see, Reg said some things that were, well, a bit crazy."

"Like what?"

"Guys, I don't know."

"Come on, Gretch, tell us."

"Fine. You really want to know?"

"Yes, as a matter of fact, I do," Uncle Uzzi insisted, and Gretchen could tell he meant it. Something about the older man made her want to trust him.

"After the sex and everything Reg sort of said he could turn into a Tiger," she said in a rush.

"I see," Uncle Uzzi said, calmly. "Did he explain what he meant?"

"He claimed he was a Shifter. I mean, he could have seen some books on my shelf earlier, but then he was saying he bit me because I'm his soulmate, or something like that, and he was shouting that I needed to let him explain but I could not take it. I didn't know what to do, so I kicked him out of my apartment, and asked him to leave me alone."

"Oh, Gretchen," Elissa said, and covered her mouth.

"He bit you?" Uncle Uzzi asked.

"Yeah. It didn't hurt at the time. In fact, it felt great," she shrugged.

Her stomach was really bothering her again. She placed a napkin over her uneaten food and put a hand to her stomach.

"Oh Gretch, you should've let him explain," Elissa began, her expression worried.

"Explain what? He's crazy Liss. People don't turn into Tigers."

"Gretchen, I need to make sure he didn't hurt you in any way," Uncle Uzzi wiped his hands with a napkin before leaning closer to Gretchen.

"No, he didn't hurt me."

"Good. Okay. What I am about to tell you is going to sound strange at first," the older man began. "But I swear to you that everything I tell you is the truth. I don't lie, Gretchen. Not ever."

"Okay," Gretchen took a second to glance at him, then at the other women.

They all wore the same sympathetic expressions

on their faces, and she couldn't for the life of her figure out why. What exactly was going on here? And what was that smell?

It was sharp and strong, and it made her nose twitch. She rubbed it with a clean napkin while listening to Uncle Uzzi. Maybe she was coming down with something, she thought as she tried to stay focused on the conversation.

"Reginald didn't lie to you, dear, and he is not crazy."

"What is he then?"

She huffed and shook her head. The smell was really bothering her, why didn't anyone else notice it? And of course, Reg was crazy. People did not turn into animals!

"Want the truth?"

Uncle Uzzi's electric blue eyes zeroed in on her, making Gretchen shiver. Still, she nodded. Yes, she wanted the truth. She'd been searching for someone special for so long, and for a moment she thought it was him. All Gretchen had ever wanted was someone to love her for who she was, flaws and all. Emailing Uncle Uzzi had been a spur-of-the-moment decision, but she knew how happy Elissa was, and yes, Gretchen had wanted some of that for herself.

She deserved the truth, especially since things moved so fast with Reg. Perhaps that was where she'd gone wrong. Either way, she never had a man make up something like that before.

*A tiger? It's nuts, right?*

Her thoughts were all jumbled. Gretchen's stomach clenched. Confusion clouded her brain as exhaustion threatened to take over. Shit, when had she become so very tired?

"Okay, Gretchen, I want you to brace yourself," Uncle Uzzi began claiming her attention once more,

"Reg really is a Shifter. A Tiger Shifter to be precise. You see Shifters exist in the real world."

"That's not possible," she said, shaking her head.

"Of course it is, Gretchen. Humans simply tend to ignore things they can't explain. I assure you Shifters are real, and Reg is one of them. If he claimed you with a bite, as you say he did, then he must be suffering greatly at this moment."

"What? Why? Did something happen to him?"

She felt alarm well up inside of her. She didn't want him hurt. Not in any way.

"Easy, there, no one has hurt him. You see, Shifters have *fated mates*. A mate is someone, or sometimes *multiple someones*, created by the universe specifically for that Shifter. They are soulmates, and a bite is what physically binds them together. Think marriage but stronger than the human ties you know of."

"So, you're saying Reg is a Tiger and I am his mate?"

Gretchen's mouth opened and closed on a dozen questions that popped in and out of her mind. Why wasn't she more upset? She wondered.

*Mine.*

A voice inside her, the same one who'd erupted in jealousy earlier, whispered inside her head. Could it be because deep down she'd known the truth? Her breathing became shallow as she tried to stem the pain rising in her stomach.

"Yes, that is what I am saying. Really, he knew better than to behave this way. I told him to tell you all this before he gave you the claiming bite and believe me when I say I will take him to task about that! I assure you I will," Uncle Uzzi said and stopped with a wide smile on his face.

He opened his arms, a gesture of peace, she knew, though why his fingertips were sparking with little lightning bolts of blue lights she had no idea. Then she heard herself and Gretchen realized she was growling at the man. And it apparently amused him.

"Excuse me," she said, and grabbed her teacup.

That certainly never happened to her before, but the second Uncle Uzzi had said he was going to yell at Reg, all these protective feelings got stirred up.

*Mine.*

"I see," Uncle Uzzi continued. "Gretchen, there are other things you should know before deciding whether you want to go through with all this."

"Like what?" Gretchen sipped her tea.

Part of her wanted to run screaming, but another part of her insisted she sit and listen. Her stomach clenched again, and suddenly, she felt very, very warm.

"Well a fated mate is the one person in the entire universe who will love you like no other. He will be unwavering in his devotion and his loyalty. You see, Shifters are not like humans. The moment he met you, and scented you, you became the most important thing in the world to Reg."

"What?"

*Could that be true?*

*Oh please, let it be true.*

"I mean it. His entire world revolves around you now, Gretchen. He will protect you, provide for you, and be there for you through thick and thin. I imagine Reg has been trying to contact you."

"Yes, he calls every couple of hours, and he's

come by, but I've avoided him," she said in a low voice.

"Gretch, are you okay?" Elissa asked, stepping forward.

Gretchen turned around to look at her best friend and felt a spark of happiness ignite inside her. Unfortunately, it was quickly squashed by a brighter flash of dizziness. Something wasn't right. She felt awful.

Maybe the food was bad? With a loud groan she collapsed to the floor, noticing everyone had backed up a few feet. Uncle Uzzi's face was concerned, but Kylie and Jessica had blanched.

"Elissa?"

"Oh. damn it. Someone, call Hunter now. Gretchen, I need you to look at me," she said.

Gretchen turned to see her friend staring at her with glowing eyes. She backed up and tried to stand, but her legs refused to cooperate. More pain coursed through her veins, like a river of lava was flowing through her instead of blood.

Everything hurt, and Gretchen was scared. She wanted Reg. She wanted her mate.

"It's gonna be okay, Gretchen. I know what's happening to you. Jessica, tell Hunter to send Reg here now."

Jessica obeyed and spoke into her cell phone. She already had it pressed to her ear when Elissa gave her the orders. Kylie had cleared away the food and was moving the furniture out of the way.

Gretchen did not know why, but she was in too much pain to think about that now. She growled, a loud animalistic sound that sent her careening down a river of hurt. More cramping followed by extreme nausea. Gretchen got to her knees and was dry heaving on the tiled floor.

"She's close," Uncle Uzzi said, and wiped her brow with a damp towel.

That felt good, but something was missing. She needed something else.

"Reggie," she whimpered, and clutched her middle before darkness claimed her.

*Mate!*

Something inside her called out to Reg. Whatever it was, whoever that voice belonged to, Gretchen instinctually trusted it would not harm her. The voice wanted Reggie and so did she.

He was the only one she wanted. The only man she had ever needed. And she needed him now.

# Chapter Fifteen

Reg paced back and forth. Even the huge living room that sat at the center of the Pride House wasn't big enough for him to walk off his agitation. He couldn't leave on the off chance she might come by to see Elissa. He couldn't change into his Tiger in case she decided to call him. He was in limbo. A fucking purgatory of his own making.

*Stupid impatient fucking shit for brains.*

It had been three days since she'd spoken to him. Three days since he'd touched her. Since he'd kissed her lips and buried himself in her heavenly body. Three long fucking days without his mate.

His Tiger scratched and snarled inside of him.

Even his beast wanted to kick his ass for fucking things up.

"Dammit!"

Reg ran his hands through his hair, but that just served to remind him of the way she'd run her fingers through it. His sweet *shona* had stood so close to him when she'd cut his hair, trying to be professional and yet unable to fight the mutual attraction that had flared to life so wildly between them.

*As it should always be between mates*, his beast recognized with a mournful whine.

She was so beautiful. Smart and funny. Taking her to dinner had been the highlight of his life. Her tiger blossom scent drove him wild, as did her heady flavors. Reg was a blessed man. Christ, he could not get her out of his head.

He wanted to track her down, get her alone in her apartment. Then he could talk some sense into her, make her believe him. After, maybe he would have the chance to lick her into orgasm after orgasm.

*Fuck.*

Once his brain went there, he couldn't stop thinking about Gretchen and what it had been like to make love to her. His cock hardened in his jeans, and he cursed his foolish impatience.

His mate was everything he'd ever wanted and more. Provocative and tempting with her many tattoos and the tiny studs in her ears. He loved those colorful highlights she'd put in her hair.

They expressed her sassy beauty in a way nothing else could. She was so confident and gorgeous. The way her pouty pink lips felt pressed against his was as close to the gods as a sinner like him could ever hope to get.

So soft and submissive, she had opened for him like a flower in bloom while maintaining an edge of dominance that left him breathless. Tender and willing, she'd given him everything, and greedy bastard that he was, Reg took.

He forgot Uncle Uzzi's advice. Forgot the one most important thing. He hadn't told her a thing about Shifters and mates. His Tiger had been riding him hard, both beast and man desperate to sink into her.

Truth was, he'd lost control. His animal side had briefly slipped into the driver's seat while he'd been loving her sweet body. He'd bitten and claimed her before he had the chance to explain anything.

A picture of Gretchen writhing on top of the

mattress they'd shared flashed through his head. Reg groaned aloud. His dick was threatening to burst a hole through the denim he wore just from thinking about her.

Great. That was all he needed.

"Reg!" Hunter called him from his office, and the younger Tiger went running.

Despite his personal problems, he'd always answer his Neta. In fact, he should probably talk to the man about what he'd done. Marking a human woman with a claiming bite was not something that should ever be done lightly, but his Tiger had been out of his mind with the need to do so.

In plain English, Reg had fucked up. Badly. But maybe, with Hunter's help, he could fix this. Reg jogged into the office to see Hunter, Brayden, and Mikey, their own Pride doc, sitting around his Neta's desk. The man himself was just putting the phone down, and he looked mad as hell.

"What went down with Gretchen Kaepernick?"

"How do you mean?"

"You know what I mean," Hunter growled the words.

Reg's fists clenched at his sides. He didn't like this. Not one bit. He didn't want to talk about Gretchen in front of his other two Pride mates. His

Tiger sure as fuck didn't want to share one sweet morsel of information about her to anyone. She was his. His alone, but even his beast recognized that he had to answer his Neta.

"She is my mate."

"I see. Did you tell her? Did you explain it to her? What it means to be mated to a Shifter and one of our Pride?"

"No, Neta. Things moved very quickly. I did explain afterwards, but she did not believe me about Shifters. I've been trying to get her to see me ever since."

"You should have tried harder," Hunter snapped.

Reg bowed his head low under the force of his Neta's Alpha voice. He was so pissed at himself he didn't even mind being forced to cower before his leader. He deserved it, and worse.

"Shit. I'm sorry Reg. My Nari is upset, and I get cranky when she is upset. Gretchen is her best friend."

"I know that. I would never do anything to hurt her. She is my whole life, Neta."

"I get it, Reg, I do."

"My Tiger is pressing hard, Neta. He wants me to go to her. It's all I can do to stop myself---"

"I understand," Hunter said and stood up.

He walked around his desk, took Reg firmly, yet gently, by the back of his neck and pressed his forehead to the younger man's. Reg submitted to his Neta's touch willingly.

There was nothing sexual or weird about it. Shifters were physical beings. In doing this, his Neta was showing his Tiger compassion, while still showing the beast Hunter was in charge.

"Be still," he growled to the Tiger, and pushed back to look at Reg with glowing teal eyes.

"I have just heard from Elissa. It looks like that love bite of yours worked a little too well. We need to go, right now. All of us."

Hunter turned to head for the door and the men followed. His words rushed through Reg's mind, but he did not understand. Something was happening. Something potentially bad.

"What is going on?"

Reg's heart thundered inside of his chest. Something was wrong. Anxiety twisted his insides, and his Tiger chuffed and snapped his jaws.

"I will explain on the way. Mikey, bring your bag, and tell Lance to come in about an hour with some men to clean up the mess."

Reg ignored Mikey who was at that moment following the Neta's instructions. He turned to

Brayden who'd offered to drive them in his enormous truck with Hunter riding shotgun.

"Neta, please tell me what is going on."

Reg's blood rushed through him, increasing his pulse, and intensifying his agitation.

"Your mate needs you, Reg," Hunter said with concern lacing his voice. "It seems she is experiencing the *Puspa*. It is dangerous, as we all know. Not everyone survives, Reg. You need to be ready."

A deafening silence filled the inside of the vehicle as Reg's brain tried to wrap around the word. Hunter's voice was laced with a combination of worry and pride. Reg couldn't have heard correctly.

*Puspa.*

His beast chuffed aloud. The Tiger was not shy about letting his own pride show through. The animal was excited and anxious to see his mate's change.

*Puspa* was from a Bengali word, the place where their type of Shifter originated. It literally meant "to blossom", but it's meaning did not end there. It was so much more to him and his Pride.

It meant Reg and Gretchen's mating was blessed by the universe. She truly was chosen for him by the Fates to share in the magic that allowed Shifters to experience life in two forms. A miracle truly. His sweet and feisty Gretchen was becoming a Shifter, like him. But it was dangerous.

*Holy fucking shit.*

Reg was a complete asshole. He hadn't explained a thing to her. She was definitely going to hate him now. Fear and sadness enveloped him like a lead blanket.

*Stop. She is our mate. We will keep her safe, make her happy.*

His Tiger's words offered some comfort, but Reg was doubtful of the welcome he'd receive. But none of that mattered right then. He was not important in the greater scheme of things. The only thing that mattered was Gretchen.

She was in pain. She would be hurt, confused, and afraid. It was his fault. All of it. Still, now was not the time for self-pity, and maybe he could help her deal with all of that.

*No.*

There was no maybe about it. Reg *would* help her. He would be there for her like he should have been in the beginning instead of thinking with his dick.

"Brayden, step on it, man," he begged the older man, refusing to give in to the anger that threatened to choke him.

He needed to be better than that. For her. A low

growl sounded from his throat as the big Bear rolled to a stop just outside of *Cut It Out*. Reg was already jumping out of the vehicle before the Bear could put it in park.

Reg scented his mate from outside the shop. Tiger blossoms and something else. Something new. Fear and pain were thick in the air, but so was the heady sweet musk of her Tiger.

*Mine,* his Tiger snarled, but Reg pressed the beast back as his Neta stepped forward.

"Let me go first," Hunter said, but Reg snapped at him.

He shook his head and took off for the door. He'd apologize to Hunter later. Right then his animal was riding him hard, holding on to control by a thread. He had to get to his mate.

His Neta raised his eyebrows, but Reg shook his head and wrenched the door open. Her scent was stronger now, and he felt her pain as if it was his own.

"Gretchen!" Her name tumbled from his lips as he saw her prone figure laid out on the floor.

She was sweaty and panting, clutching her stomach while the other women crowded her. That was no good. She needed space.

"Please, back up," he growled, and four pairs of eyes zeroed in on him.

"Well," Uncle Uzzi said. "Her mate is here. Let's go, ladies, give him room."

"Reg, take care of her." Elissa looked at him with tears in her warm brown eyes, and he nodded helplessly. He would try.

Hunter pushed past him to help his Nari stand, but Reg hardly registered the move. He was trying to calm his Tiger's need to snarl and snap at everyone in the room. He wanted his mate.

*Alone.*

With a supportive arm around her waist, Hunter led Elissa to a chair and stood by her side. Reg looked at him and his Neta nodded. It was his turn now to help his mate.

"Reggie," Gretchen whimpered, and turned her head towards him though her eyes remained firmly shut.

Sweat dotted her brow, as she clutched her middle and moaned aloud.

"I'm here, *shona*," he said, and watched as she extended a hand to him.

*Thank the fucking gods.*

Reg took it in his and held on tightly. Hope erupted through him like a volcano. She opened those baby blues that he loved so much and looked at him for one second before glancing behind him. Reg turned around and snarled. Mikey was there, hands raised as if in surrender.

"Reg, I have to check her vitals, to see how she's doing," Mikey said.

The reasonable part of Reg understood the necessity, but his Tiger wanted to rip the fucker to shreds. He nodded his ascent but could do nothing to stop himself from growling as the man reached over.

First, Mikey felt her forehead, then checked her pupils, and lastly, put two fingers on her throat to check her pulse. Gretchen whimpered, and tried to bat him away, but she was too weak to do much.

"Stop. Not you. Don't touch me. Only Reggie," Gretchen moaned and shook her head back and forth.

Reg reached out and grasped her hand, shouldering Mikey out of the way.

"Stop it. She doesn't want you touching her," Reg growled, and Mikey backed up immediately. Smart man.

"Okay, alright. Look Reg, this is definitely the *Puspa*, but she isn't reacting the way Elissa did."

"How do you mean?"

"This is new to me. Elissa is the only other person I have ever seen go through this. Maybe it is because you aren't an Alpha pair."

"So?" Reg grabbed Mikey by the shirt and shook him. "Tell me what that means! What are you saying?" he cried out, tears of fury escaped his eyes as he released his friend.

"Her pulse is weak. She is tiring. I don't know what to do. I'm sorry," Mikey told him, shame, and sadness in his eyes.

Reg refused to accept what his friend said. He dropped back to the floor, next to his mate and shook his head. Wiping her brow with a wet hand-kerchief that he found next to her, Reg started talking to her.

Nonsense words and apologies at first. Random things that they'd talked about on their one date. He whispered anything and everything he could to keep her from fading. Gretchen moaned again and clutched her stomach.

A wave of tremors caused her to shudder and gasp. He tuned out everyone else in the room. He heard their gasps and his Nari's tears, but Reg couldn't concentrate on them. They were not important in that moment.

Someone handed him a pillow, and he lifted her

head and placed it beneath. She whimpered in response and flailed about until he took her hand. Her breathing was heavy and pained, it was all he could do not to break down. Tears fell from his eyes, but he didn't care. This was his mate, and it was because of him that she was suffering. He listened helplessly as her heartbeat slowed.

"Mikey!" he yelled for his Pride mate and their healer. "Help her! Please!"

His cries echoed in the salon as his friend rushed to his side. Mikey checked her over. Doing all the things Reg would expect of a doctor, but it didn't seem to help. She was still fading. The minutes ticked by like hours, but they were still no closer to an answer.

"I am sorry, Reg," Mikey began. "I just don't know how this will work. If it will work out."

"Don't say that, of course it will. You're strong, *shona*, show him how strong," Reg said to her, kissing her hand. He squeezed it, hating how weak and limp it was.

"She seems to be fighting it, fighting her Tiger, and I don't know what happens if she does, but it can't be good," Mikey said, and the healer couldn't meet Reg's eyes.

"No," gasped Elissa from somewhere behind them. Everyone else in the room went quiet.

Reg's heart beat inside his chest like mad. Everything in him, his Tiger especially, rejected what Mikey said. This couldn't be right. This couldn't be it.

He turned to Gretchen. He could scent her fear and confusion. The fact that she was in pain because of him because he'd put her in that position, was tearing him apart.

"Reg, I'm so sorry," Mikey spoke, and Reg threw his head back and roared out loud.

He'd only just found her. Gretchen was his mate to love and cherish, to protect and care for. There was no fucking way she was going to die. He wouldn't allow it.

"No. You're wrong. She's going to get through this," he said, and turned to his mate.

Reg ripped away the blanket and the pillow. He wanted her awake, not complacent. Maybe even angry. Hell, he could take her anger. He could take anything if she just woke up.

He turned her face to his and dropped a kiss on her brow, holding her with two hands on her cheeks before speaking intently.

"Gretchen, you have to listen to me. Get up,

*shona.* I know you're scared and angry right now. I know you don't want to see me anymore, and I don't blame you. I fucked up. I did this, but you are not a coward. You are not going to lay down and die because of my fuck up, now open your eyes!" Reg growled at her weak whimpered response.

"Get up, baby. Wake up. Let your Tiger in. She is part of you now. You are stronger than ever before, now show me. Show me how fucking strong you are, *shona.* I know you are pissed, and you deserve to be. I promise you, Gretchen, I will let you kick my ass later. I will even try to leave you alone if that is what you want. But not till you get the fuck up. You hear me? After this is all finished, I will take a ship to fucking Antarctica, if you want me to," Reg told her.

She whimpered, the movement behind her eyelids picking up pace. She didn't like it when he yelled at her, and he could have laughed. But he was not about to stop. Not when he needed her so damn bad. Without her, he didn't think he could go on living.

"Stop fighting your Tiger, baby, and listen to me. Remember how good it was when I stripped you bare and kept your heels on, *shona?* I remember. I remember everything, the way you tasted, the way you smelled, fuck, I love your smell, and the way you felt wrapped around me like hot, wet, silk. The way your pussy squeezed me when you came and fuck, you were so beautiful, like a goddess. I love you, Gretchen, I love you so much. Now Shift to your Tiger. Let her take over for now and after that you can have anything you want," he pleaded and begged with her. Reg really didn't care who was there to witness him breaking down at that point.

"The pain you feel is your body changing. You are growing, blossoming into something else," he took a fortifying breath and looked to his Pride mates, to worthy males like Hunter, Brayden, and even Mikey.

They stood there for him offering silent support as did the females in the room who nodded at him to continue.

"Gretchen, you are turning into a Shifter, like me. Your Tiger is a part of you now. Just like your tattoo, but deep inside. She is part of your soul, and she will give you strength even as she takes it now to transform you. Let her in, Gretchen, you have to let her in. I know I should have explained better. I am so sorry, *shona*, I should have done so many things differently. I should have waited, tried harder to explain," his voice cracked, and he wiped his eyes.

"Hurts, hurts bad," she cursed and rolled to her side.

Reg barked a laugh through his tears. She was talking! That was good, right?

"I know, *shona.* I'm so sorry it hurts, but you can do this."

"Did you just tell everyone what we did, Reggie?"

"Sorry baby, it couldn't be helped."

"Owwwww!" she roared, the pain taking hold.

"You're so strong, so brave. Close your eyes, Gretchen, look inside yourself. Can you see her? Can you see your Tiger?"

"I see her, Reggie," she whimpered.

"She won't hurt you. She is part of you. Just let her in. Accept her and all the pain will go away. Come on, love. You got this. I swear you got this, baby," he said, wishing like hell he could take some of her pain away.

Eventually, Gretchen stopped groaning and with a burst of energy that had him jumping back, he watched as she rolled over onto all fours. Her fingers scratched at her clothes, and she tore through the fabric of her top like it was nothing, but her pants and shoes were not as easy.

Reg turned his head and bared his teeth to the men in the room. Yes, they were Shifters and used to nudity, but this was his mate. She deserved some privacy.

The men averted their gazes, and he allowed his claws to descend so he could help tear through his mate's clothes.

*"Regggrrrrrrrrooooowwwwwllll!"*

His name turned into a long growl as ripples of magic wracked her tiny frame. Reg moved back, giving her space. He was completely awestruck as bones began to break, muscles tore, and flesh ripped and reformed.

Her human half fell away and, a few minutes later, his beautiful mate twisted and turned into a powerful, majestic Tiger right before his eyes.

Her animal was smaller than his, but so gorgeous. Four-hundred pounds of kick-ass feline hissed and spat at the room.

Perspiration dotted her she-Cat's fur, but he didn't dare touch her yet. He recalled his own painful first transformation, and Reg knew it would be a moment before her skin would lose its sensitivity.

Hands flexed at his side, he took in her gorgeous form instead. Her striped coat was a thick and glossy shade of orange, just a tad darker than his own. She had a long tail with a tuft of white fur just on the end.

Gretchen grumbled and flashed her four-inch

long canines while stretching her claws, tearing the blanket on the floor to shreds in the process.

*Shit.*

He hoped she wasn't going to be too pissed at the damage her feline was causing.

*Fuck it.*

He would replace everything. It was the least he could do. Her first steps were wobbly, and she started to slide, but Reg caught her easily. He helped her to stand, laughing when she hissed and spat at him.

"Always so feisty," he said and smiled.

His mate's Tiger turned and sniffed the air around him. She sneezed, then shook her head and took a step closer to Reg. Already on his knees, he held out a tentative hand. The last thing he wanted was to startle her. Shifters healed quickly, that was true, but even he couldn't grow back a limb should his mate decide to snap off a finger, *or five* with her enormous teeth.

Fuck. She was gorgeous even in her fur.

He waited a beat until, finally, his *shona* leaned into his touch. Soft fur and heat seeped through his fingers and Reg exhaled the breath he'd been holding.

Gretchen chuffed and rubbed her head against

him affectionately, marking him with her scent. The beast recognized him as her mate, causing a smile to break out across his face. Gretchen continued to circle him, rubbing her furry self against him, wherever she could reach. Chest, back, arms, face, legs, continuing to leave him covered in her tiger lily scent.

He fucking loved it, and his big Cat purred in response. Reg dropped his head onto her back and inhaled deeply. The flowery scent unique to her was more profound in this form, and he savored the opportunity to breathe her in.

His mate turned her Tiger's head and licked him, her large sandy tongue swapping at his cheek and chin. Reg laughed again. His whole focus was on her even as his friends and Pride mates celebrated behind him.

"Go, run with your mate," Hunter told him, and for the first time he felt true fear rise inside him.

"She may not want me as a mate," Reg replied in a voice. The thought broke his heart.

"Reg, this is not the time for such a decision. True, things should have been handled differently, but forget that now. Why don't you and your mate do as your Neta says?" Uncle Uzzi clucked and walked to the back door to open it.

Gretchen looked at him, her Tiger eyes the same sky blue as her human form, before she turned to the door. He could tell she needed to go and explore the world in this shape. One glance back at him, and his sweet mate chuffed and nodded.

*Thank the gods.*

He began to disrobe, dropping his clothes where he stood as he joined her in his fur. With any luck this would be the first of many such nights, He thought before following his beautiful mate outside.

*I'm gonna be the man you deserve, shona. I promise.*

Reg vowed before taking off after her.

# Chapter Sixteen

*oly furry fucking butt sniffing shit balls!*

Gretchen could not believe this. Shifters were real, and thanks to getting down and dirty with a certain smexy as fuck guy who was a Tiger in the sack, and apparently, out of it, she now had fur. And a tail. And claws. And big ass teeth.

Well, her new, huge ass Tiger did. She'd first seen the beautiful she-Cat stalking around inside her head. But the thing that was difficult to understand was the Tiger was her.

Sort of. Metaphysically speaking.

*Gulp.*

*Okay.*

*What the actual fuck?*

She'd been on the floor, trying to cower and hide from the pain when a familiar voice had demanded she get her ass in gear and face it. Man, was he fucking annoying! Stupid male, ordering her around. Who the heck did he think he was?

*He is our mate. But we can still bite his ass.*

Oh fuck, she gulped. Now she was going crazy! Who knew that shit was contagious?

*Don't be scared. I am you now.*

Um. Say what?

*You are going through the Puspa. It is a blessing revered by our kind. I am your animal spirit. Soon you shall be able to change forms between Tiger and human. Embrace me, little one. Together we can greet our mate, and those of our Pride who are gathered around us even now.*

Easy for that furry little beyotch to say. She was sitting in some ethereal plane with glowing lights and fantasy trees and shit. Gretchen was in the grips of the worst pain she had ever felt. It hurt worse than having her wisdom teeth pulled, and that time she'd had an ovarian cyst pop. Both had required serious painkillers to see her through.

*All change comes with a little pain, but you are strong. Listen to our mate. See how he encourages us? He is a good male.*

Good? Gretchen would have laughed if she wasn't dying. That bastard was the one who did this to her. Fucker came into her life swinging that big dick of his, and he didn't even tell her he turned into a freaky ass Tiger.

*Grrrr.*

Fine, Tigers were not freaky, and Reg was all kinds of beautiful. But she was not ready for this. Couldn't he have softened the blow somehow? Gretchen argued with the beast in her head for what seemed like forever.

Finally, after listening to Reg's sweet pleading, and his angrier ones, she came to a realization. The she-Cat had a point. But how could Gretchen just accept this fantasy for fact? She didn't believe in things like Shifters. Those were just stories. Make believe stuff and nonsense like the creatures in those naughty, little books she read on her phone between cutting and dying her clients' hair.

*Oh shit.*

She groaned as another round of pain hit her right in the gut. Shifters were real, and she'd taken one to bed. No wonder she'd attacked him like an animal. She was one. Or well, she was one now.

*Because of him and his stupid stripey though totally hot ass--- Ooowww! Ouchie!*

Okay, pain aside, she wasn't sure how she actually felt about this. Her Tiger had confirmed what everyone kept saying. Reggie was in fact her mate. A fated mate at that, which was something blessed by the universe, and the gods, of which she was getting a feeling there were multiple.

*Mate. Hmm.*

The word felt strange, and yet, familiar somehow as it rolled around her brain. Her heart was pounding heavily, the muscle working to keep her alive while she fought the inevitable. Gretchen growled, the sound of her own blood roaring in her ears making it near impossible to think.

She wanted Reg, but could she trust him? That was the real question. Her inner feline claimed he was a good male, but she didn't know him well enough to make that kind of judgement. He'd lied by omission. How was that good?

He did try to explain though, and she had been less than willing to cooperate. Okay, she flat out refused to listen to anything he had to say over the past few days. But this was huge. This was her whole life on the line.

*Pros and cons, okay, here we go.*
*Pros:*

Reg was undeniably gorgeous, Gretchen could

not deny her physical attraction to him. He made her body hum with pleasure just from being near him. He was also funny, charming, and a good listener. He made her feel good about herself and seemed to really care when she spoke about her work and hoped for the future. And there was that purring thing he did when he had her clit in his mouth. A girl had to count that.

*Cons:*

Reg totally fucking lied about being able to turn into a big ass Cat. Did anything else matter after that one? Oh yeah, and he bit her and changed her into a big ass Cat without permission.

*Grrr.*

Her Tiger didn't exactly like being called that, but as far as she was concerned, Miss Kitty could stuff it or no catnip for her!

*Damn.*

How could she make such a huge decision without more info? Blinding pain shot through her again in great, powerful waves, until she felt as if she'd been swept away by them.

It was like being caught in a riptide. It was happening all too fast, and she had zero control. Gretchen's body was burning, she was on fire. She felt like she was being torn in two. She tried breathing, but she could hardly stand it.

Someone was touching her, talking some more, but she didn't want that. It was not Reg, and that was not okay. She only wanted his hands on her. No one else. She stumbled trying to get away. She was suffocating, but there was nothing she could do to stop it.

Then suddenly, she scented him near. Reg was there with her. His warm, strong hands enveloped hers. He was talking to her, whispering words of encouragement, begging her to stay and fight.

Of course, she would. Did he think she was dying?

*Oh my gah!*

*Was she dying?*

Fear spiked through her heart, and she felt herself gasping. Her blood was like cement, and she wasn't getting any air.

*No. Let me in, little one. I can make the pain stop, just let go and give yourself over to me.*

Her Tiger pleaded with her, but she was still so afraid. Then Reg was there once more, whispering to her fiercely.

*"She won't hurt you. She is part of you. Just let her in. Accept her and all the pain will go away. Come on, love.*

*You got this. I swear you got this, baby,"* his voice was thick with emotion, and Gretchen's heart swelled.

*Mate. Mine.*

Her Tiger roared ferociously, and Gretchen let go of her grip on that plane of reality. Fire burned through her veins, the sounds of bones cracking and muscles stretching then reknitting filled her oh-so-sensitive ears.

It felt like an eternity, but it was only minutes until she went from lying on her back to wobbling on four paws. She blinked slowly through her new eyes. The world seemed different, askew, but clear. Very clear.

*Oh shit. I'm a Tiger. I'm a fucking Tiger! Hear me ROAR!*

Gretchen turned to her mate and hissed. Did she hear him right? Did that fucker say he would leave her if she wanted?

Hell to the no. He was not going anywhere, certainly not away from her. Not now. She didn't want him gone. Not at all. The man deserved a little ass kicking, but she would save that for later. Just then, her paws itched to run.

She hissed and chuffed at him, flicking him in the face with her tail before bounding over to the back-door that Uncle Uzzi was currently holding wide open.

She stopped and blinked slowly at the sly old man. No, *sniff,* not just an old man. Uncle Uzzi was something else, something magical or so her new senses told her.

The white haired man who was a friend simply smiled and winked at Gretchen. The feline growled lightly before taking off down the street, and into the forest that waited just beyond an old church off the main stretch of road.

She didn't have to use her new senses to know it was her mate who stalked behind her. Gretchen felt it, *felt him,* deep inside her heart. A growl began in her chest, but it sounded more like a purr to her.

*Reggie.*

Her mind reached out for him, searching past the gold and silver tendrils of magic that seemed interwoven between this plane and the next.

*Pride bonds,* her instincts told her. She found one thin silvery one and followed it. She wondered why it was so warm and bright, growing brighter still as she watched and traced it until, suddenly, Reg was there.

*Mate.* His deep gravelly voice replied, echoing in her head and filling Gretchen's heart with joy.

She stilled, watching him step forward through the darkness to where she waited in a small grassy clearing. His Tiger was truly a magnificent specimen. Regal and proud, double the size of her own beast.

Still, he proceeded with caution. Unsure of his welcome. That was not okay with her beast. Her Tiger stretched her neck, assuming a haughty pose and watched him go still before she pounced.

She might be new to being a Tiger, but some things were pure instinct. Right now, she wanted him to chase her. After she'd leapt onto his back, she bounded off, hissing and chuffing at him. Gretchen ran away from him in circles and zigzags.

*So, you want to play? Alright little she-Cat, but I'm warning you, I always win.*

Her mate's voice spoke clearly in her head, and she laughed at the wonder and magic of it all.

*You wish, pal. You're not catching this Tiger by the tail.*

Gretchen growled at him before racing off into the woods, but not before she heard his reply.

*Challenge accepted, shona. Come here kitty, kitty.*

# Chapter Seventeen

After an hour of running about the forest, chasing his fiery little mate, Reg had to admit defeat.

"*Who* always wins?" she asked.

Gretchen came out of her bathroom still damp from the quick shower she took. She was wearing nothing but a bath sheet, but suddenly, she appeared very conscious of that fact.

Must be the way Reg was staring at her. Like if he looked hard enough, he could see right through the thing.

*He fucking wished.*

She gulped and pulled it tighter. Fuck. He knew they needed to talk, even though all he wanted was to jump on her and have her ride him till the sun came up.

His chest rumbled as he watched her from his position on her couch, wearing the jeans he'd left behind in her salon. Nerves on edge, he'd stopped breathing the second she entered the room.

*Holy fuck.*

Was it possible she'd grown even more beautiful in a matter of days? His body reacted predictably, and he refused to hide it. It was a bloody fucking miracle. This kind of heat and need always was.

Reg wanted her. He always would. In fact, his attraction seemed to grow by the second.

"Me," he answered her question, and smiled at her confused expression. "You might have won the game, *shona*, but if I still get to be here with you when the game has ended, then I am the winner."

"Oh," she replied, swallowing, and looking down. Fuck, she'd painted her toes purple, and Reg grinned. Even her feet were cute.

"You've called me that before. *Shona.* What does it mean?"

"Oh, um, it's a term of endearment. Though probably only used by our Pride. It's a Bangla word, passed down through our families and traditions, like our Tigers themselves," he began and felt his cheeks grow warm as he explained. "It means *sweet-heart* or *darling*."

"I like it. And that's fascinating, I would like to learn more about your family and ancestors, Reg."

"I'll tell you anything you want to know, *shona*. Anytime you want," he murmured, his blood rushing through his veins like thunder in his ears.

His mate approached him slowly and stealthily across the room until she was standing directly in front of him. The flowery scent of her skin made his mouth drool as did imagining her naked beneath the robe.

"Gretchen," he whispered her name.

The one word was infused with so much longing, but he didn't dare touch her. Not yet. If he did, he would not be able to stop. It was hard admitting that kind of loss of control, even to himself. But if he was *Superman*, she would be his *Kryptonite*.

Yes, she'd frolicked and played with him while in her fur. Also true, they were fated mates. But he would not force or cajole her into being with him. She had to make the decision herself.

He knew if he touched her, it would take the choice away from both of them. Fated mates and physical attraction went hand in hand. But he wanted her for much more than her sweet body.

He could not make the first move. Not Reg. He could not touch her yet. That would ruin any chance they had for a future.

*Fucking kill me now,* he thought and closed his eyes breathing forcefully through his nose.

Of course, it might have been easier had he just cut off his hands. Her flowery scent filled his nostrils and shot right to his groin. Droplets of water clung to her hair and her skin was pink and fresh from her shower. She was temptation itself. And Reg was a dead man.

"Why are your eyes closed?"

"Because if I look at you any longer, I'll have to touch you, *shona,* and right now that is not what you need from me."

"What do I need from you?" she asked, and he thought he felt a swoosh of air in front of him, but he kept his eyes closed tightly.

"Time. Answers. Just ask me or tell me what you want to know. Whatever it is you want, I will do it or get it for you," he replied.

"Open your eyes and look at me, Reggie," she whispered, and he obeyed, opening his eyes slowly.

Reg nearly lost the ability to speak once he came face to face with his mate in all her glory. Gretchen was biting her lower lip, standing before him like some kind of offering. The bath sheet she'd had on lay in a puddle at her feet.

She was naked and glowing from her bath, mere inches from him. Bare, bold, and beautiful.

*Mine*, snarled his Tiger.

"Mate," he growled the word, and fisted his hands tightly at his sides. "You're not making it easy to be noble, *shona*."

"I don't want you to be noble, Reggie. I just want *you*. I want to feel you deep inside of me, right now, Reg. Need you, mate," she purred the words, and his cock throbbed in response.

That was all he needed to hear. Without further delay or hesitation, Reg scooped Gretchen off her feet, lifting her by her luscious hips. She complied immediately by wrapping her legs around his waist, pressing her hot wet sex against his belly. His already hard cock throbbed with need.

*Fuck*, she was so very wet, and he wanted her so damn badly. He mashed his mouth to hers. Locking her plump lips with his and nibbling on the lower one.

*Grrrr.*

His Tiger wanted more. He wanted it all.

Reg focused on the kiss. The mouth was a funny

orifice. A person ate with it. Drank with it. Spoke with it. And then there was kissing.

Kissing was something else. Something entirely intimate, that allowed him to be both the aggressor and completely vulnerable. He never really enjoyed kissing before. But with her, Reg loved it.

He really *really* loved it. Kissing her was beyond anything he'd ever experienced. Christ, that mouth. It was fucking gorgeous. Those pouty pink lips were so ripe, so tasty, *purrfect* for kissing.

Gretchen liked it too. He knew from the way she opened for him with sweet reckless abandon, completely trusting in him to take care of her. Her softly delivered submission had his Tiger snarling and his body wound tight. Reg wanted to be balls deep and surrounded by her.

Fuck, he was ready to spend hours just kissing the woman, but then she wiggled. His impatient little *shona* raked her nails down his back and slapped his ass, urging him on. Reg growled, his eyes glowing with his beast. Her needs came first. Always.

If his little she-Cat wanted more, he would give it to her. They collapsed on the bed with Reg kicking off his jeans. His mouth quickly dropping back down to claim her lips once more.

"Need you, mate," she groaned and tugged on his bottom lip with her sharp teeth.

Of course, her own beast would be riding her hard. Her she-Tiger would want to confirm their mating, and he was more than ready to give her anything, everything she ever wanted.

"Mine," he snarled like some kind of fucking cave-Tiger, but he did not give a fuck.

He was a possessive ass, but she was his, and he reminded her of that fact by grazing his teeth along her neck. Reg scraped his fangs over her healed mating mark. Loving the way, she wiggled and squirmed beneath him.

He grinned wickedly and did it again. That little spot would always be special between them. A physical trigger for an emotional bond that would only grow and grow to untold heights.

That was only if she wanted it to. Fuck, he really hoped she wanted it to.

Gretchen wiggled again, her soft wet heat rubbing against the hard bar of his cock. He hissed out a long breath. She felt so good. Soft, supple, and submissive, and yet she fiercely dominant, egging him on with her pants and nips and moans. Tugging and pulling, pleading, and demanding until he touched her where she wanted.

*So totally fucking hot.*

He was putty in her hands.

*If putty was a hard as steel rod,* his inner beast growled.

Reg's cock jerked in her hands, and Reg growled as she reached between them and cupped his balls while massaging his shaft.

"Lie back," she commanded, flipping their positions.

Reg obeyed, turning until he was sitting on the bed with his back against the headrest. His sexy mate stared at him with glowing blue eyes. It seemed her Tiger wanted in on this.

*Fuck yeah,* that was more than okay with him. It meant, if he was lucky, she might claim his sorry ass.

Reg growled and licked his lips as Gretchen knelt between his splayed legs. Her heavy breasts swayed back and forth, a delight for his eyes, and his mouth watered with longing.

"Not yet, big boy, first I get to play," she said, and leaned down to lick a trail from the base of his cock all the way to the dewy drop of precum that leaked from his slit.

"Fuck," he growled, watching intently as she continued to lick and fondle.

He'd never seen anything as gorgeous as

Gretchen making long swipes with the flat side of her tongue along his aching cock. She was so fucking hot, paying close attention to the thick vein that throbbed with desire for her and her alone.

His mate adjusted her position, and with a sly wink she took him in her mouth, swallowing him down until he hit the back of her throat.

"Oh fuck, *shona*. S'good," he grunted, and growled as she sucked him down far as she could, sliding her lips along his base and leaving a shiny trail of saliva in her wake.

Searing arousal tore through him as he thrust inside her mouth. Reg knew he was a dead man the second she wrapped her hands around the base of his cock, using one to fondle his balls tenderly while she sucked and squeezed until he was nearly out of his mind.

*Fuck,* he couldn't stop his orgasm, though he tried.

Okay, not very hard, but he did try to resist. Reg was a goner.

"Gimme," she growled with her mouth full of cock.

And he did. He gave up all control to his mate, but fuck, what a way to go! She slid her palm up and down along the base of his dick, in time with the hot suction of her mouth. Using her tongue to lap and caress his head, until fuck, he was going to blow.

Balls tightened, gasping for air, Reg held her head in place, fucking her mouth until he felt the first spikes of pleasure start to form.

"Gonna come, *shona*, you gotta let go," he warned, but she tightened her hold, and shook her head.

Working double time, she looked up at him with glowing sky blue eyes. He felt her growl reverberate from her body through to his cock, felt her sharp claws pierce his thigh, and that was it for him.

Reg tossed his head back, a roar escaping his lips as he chased his orgasm, stroking the caverns of her hot mouth until he came to completion.

Tendrils of ecstasy shot through him starting from his cock and spiraling out all the way to his fingertips and toes. Reg came inside her mouth, and his gorgeous mate swallowed down every last drop of his release.

Tiny aftershocks pulsed through him, but still, his mate held on. His sexy she-Cat refused to let go of her prize. Licking and stroking, his sexy as hell mate caressed his dick tenderly, taking every drop of his cum inside of her.

Gretchen sat up slowly, licking her expert lips and smiling like the cat who swallowed the canary.

*Fuck yeah*, she sure did. His fiery little mate had sucked him dry.

"Mine," she growled.

Reg would have thought he was utterly spent, but *surprise surprise*. His dick stood up and saluted the beauty who just brought him to heaven and back. He growled, grabbing his revived hard on.

He loved her possessive statement--- no, fuck that, Reg loved *her*. So damn much. And he wanted to show her. It wouldn't take long. He could probably do it in another fifty or sixty years.

"That's right, *shona*, I'm all yours. Now, it's my turn. I want you face down on the bed, mate," he demanded.

Her eyes widened, but he could tell her Cat like the sound of that, and down she went. Sweet little ass held high, his mate moaned as she lay face down on the mattress like a good little kitten.

Only his kitten was a fierce as fuck Tiger. And Reg was one lucky male.

*Grrr.*

Reg leaned forward and spread her legs, dropping his palm down hard on one rip globe. She mewled at the sting, but he made up for it with a wet kiss over her reddening skin.

"Gonna lick you now, mate," he told her and

dipped down, diving right in. Reg loved feasting on her sweet cream, and from this angle it gave him a clear path from her clit to her sweet little forbidden hole.

There was nothing in the world compared to the flavor of his mate's arousal. Heady and strong, her flowery musk had him salivating for more. Gretchen cried and bucked while he sucked down her salty, sweet essence.

She was more than ready for him. Moisture dripped from her slit, and he gladly lapped up every sweet drop. Later, he would take her ass, but for now he was all about going deep and hard into her tight channel.

"Gonna take you now, Gretchen. Gonna fill you with my cock. Fuck you so good, mate," he growled, kneeling behind her, and parting her folds with his thick head.

Back and forth he rubbed, teasing her mercilessly. He nudged her clit with that broad head, then he retreated. Again and again, he used his thick length to stroke her outer lips, brushing against her sensitive bundle of nerves until she snarled and turned around, her eyes glowing with her animal.

Fuck, that was so hot.

"Stop fucking around," she growled, but Reg smirked his reply.

"Patience," he told her, slapping that sweet ass one more time.

He was in charge here. She tried to press back, but he held her still with a firm hand on her hip. He loved the heart shaped curve of her ass, teased her there again with his thumb, while brushing his cock along her slit, coating himself in her juices.

Everything about her drove him crazy with desire. When he'd teased them both long enough, and had her mewling incoherently, Reg filled her with a single fierce thrust of his cock thrust and pressed his thumb deep inside her asshole.

"Mine," Reg growled, his invasion deep and thorough.

This position made it easier for him to determine the speed and strength of his movements. He wanted it to last, wanted her moaning and bucking beneath him.

So, Reg started slowly, relishing each sweet inch of her slick channel, her ass squeezing his thumb as her pussy did his cock.

His *shona* was impatient, she pushed back taking him deeper and faster than he'd intended. That earned her another slap on her cheek. He knew she liked the sting, could tell by the way her pussy clenched around him.

He could scent her arousal spike and he growled wickedly. His little mate liked it when he spanked her. Like his finger in her ass and his cock in her pussy. That was good, he thought as he slapped her ass again, her pussy and anus clenching around him once more, eliciting a groan from both of them. He liked it too.

"Mine, *shona*. You are mine," Reg growled and moved.

He played with her ass some more, loving her squirms, before withdrawing. Later, he would take her there later, he growled and collapsed forward, caging her in on all sides. He needed both hands for this.

The time for going slow was over. Reg withdrew from her heat and slammed forward. Harder, faster, deeper. He pounded into her furiously, bringing them both to greater heights than he'd ever reached.

"Mine," he repeated, and reached round to find her hard, swollen clit.

"Yours," she echoed, working with him, fighting for release.

Reg's fangs descended. He strummed the nubbin with his forefinger and roared as her pussy squeezed his cock even tighter. He could not hold back any longer.

"Gonna mark you," he growled.

"Yes," she returned, her gaze holding his as he struck through her skin with his sharp fangs.

Teeth slicing through the skin on the back of her shoulder, Reg drank down her life's force. He scored her hips with his claws too, but he was careful not to mar the beautiful tattoo that graced his mate's luscious curves. His orgasm ripped through him, as their mate bond wrapped around them.

Reg held nothing back. He just kept fucking her as he spilled his seed deep inside her womb. Gretchen's orgasm raced through her, but his sweet shona still turned her head. Mashing her lips to his, he hissed loudly when she nudged his face aside and latched onto his shoulder, biting him with her own sharp fangs.

*Oh sweet fuck, she was marking him as her own!*

Reg's orgasm grew and grew until he thought he would die from it. So much pleasure, he never thought it was possible.

They were both hoarse from roaring by the time they collapsed onto the mattress, his cock still buried deep inside her sweet pussy. They lay in a sweaty and sticky tangle, boneless and completely sated, neither one of them could move.

Still, he could not stop the grin from spreading across his face, even as he sucked in air greedily. He couldn't help it. She'd marked him. Really marked him good judging from the sting. Reg was too damn tired, to turn his head and look.

She'd claimed him as her own for all the world to see, and he had never been happier in his whole life. His Tiger roared with pride even as his cock continued to pulse.

He was insatiable for her. A marrow deep satisfaction coursed through him. Whatever this had been, too impulsive, too soon again, it didn't matter because it felt right. Primal and raw, their sex had been life changing.

He was whole and complete. Why shouldn't he be? He was well and truly claimed by his mate.

*And wasn't that a-fucking-mazing?*

Reg's chest vibrated with the strength of his purr as she sighed against the arms he had wrapped around her. Pure bliss echoed through him, filling the room with warmth and the heady scent of their mating sex.

He could spend forever wrapped around her, he

thought, and happily too, tending to her every need and want. He'd give her lifetimes if she let him.

"Mine," he whispered once more as he fell asleep like that, balls deep inside his mate.

It was the only place he ever wanted to be, he thought as the spring sun peeked through the blinds, warming their satiated bodies.

*Mate.*

# Chapter Eighteen

Gretchen grinned at her last client, a wonderfully blunt elderly woman who'd wanted her to dye the tips of her short hair bright pink for her grandbaby's fourth birthday.

"Maia wants a fairy princess party, and I told her I would be ready for it. She is gonna love this," Mrs. Sanchez said, and patted Gretchen's hand affectionately.

"I just bet she will Mrs. Sanchez," Gretchen told the woman as she put the last finishing touches on her new do.

She watched the clock anxiously as she wrote up the bill. Tara, a teenaged girl she'd hired to work the reception desk on the weekends, rang her up while Gretchen walked over to the window.

"I'm just gonna grab some lunch," she told the teen as Reg pulled up to the curb.

She was in such a good mood lately. Heck, she even giggled when Marion made an obscene gesture, and fanned himself as Reg hopped out of the driver's seat and stalked over to her.

"Cut it out," she yelled, laughing as everyone groaned at the pun. It was the name of her establishment, after all. She wagged her finger at Marion before racing out the door and tackling Reg.

Her fine as fuck mate caught her easily and slammed his mouth to hers. The kiss was hot and quick. Too quick in her opinion, but she'd learned the hard way that was best.

If one of them didn't put a stop to their kisses quickly, they'd end up naked in seconds no matter where they were. It had already happened in the bathroom, the kitchen, the stairwell, and even the rather cramped back seat of his Jeep.

*Sigh.*

*Oh, her aching vagina.*

She thought he broke the damn thing last night. But they were all good aches, she smiled slyly and thanked heaven for Shifter healing and rejuvenation abilities.

"My employees think you're hot," she told Reg as

he squeezed her from behind while she opened the door to the stairwell that led to her apartment.

"Yeah? And what do you think?" he asked and kissed her on the neck.

"I think you're okay," she shrugged, then laughed uncontrollably as he mock-growled, and nuzzled her mating mark while tickling her belly.

"Oh fuck, stop it or I am gonna trip up the stairs," she said, knowing he would let her go immediately if there was a chance she was going to get hurt.

She'd learned that Shifters, especially mated ones, were very protective of their significant others. Reg was a complete and total doll. Her sexy tattooed mate would do anything for her, and wonder of wonders, she felt the same. It was so fast, true, but she had never felt so good in her life.

Gretchen ran up the stairs with him following closely behind her. That was another thing she'd learned. Running from a predator almost always ensured getting chased. Something she liked, but only if Reg was doing the chasing.

After a few more quick kisses at her insistence, Reg sat down at the table, and she went to the fridge. She'd wanted to surprise him with lunch today. Gretchen bit her lip as she pulled out some home-made chicken salad sandwiches.

"I made these for us," she said, and laughed at his shocked expression. "What? I can cook."

"Wow. I just didn't expect this. Thank you, *shona*."

"Well, after living with Elissa, I picked up a few things."

"I love chicken salad," he said, and ate more than half of the sandwich in two bites.

"Mm, good," he managed with his mouth full.

Gretchen giggled and wiped his mouth with her napkin. That just got her another sloppy wet kiss she absolutely loved. Shit, there was that word again.

*Love.*

It made her nervous and gooey inside. A bundle of anxiety if she were being truthful. Did mates love each other? Was that a thing for Shifters? There was so much she did not know.

After they'd finished eating, she handed him a tall glass of water with a slice of lemon floating on top. Reg winked at her and tipped it to his lips. She sighed, marveling at how he drank the entire thing in one sip.

*My oh my*, she loved a man with a big appetite.

Okay. Truth time. She loved *this man* and all of his appetites. She just hadn't told him yet. Being his mate was fine and good. Hell, more than that. It was better than she had ever expected, but he never said a thing about love.

Her heart squeezed at the thought that he could grow tired of her one day. After all, even if Uncle Uzzi and Elissa were telling the truth when they'd said a mate was the epitome of devotion, neither of them mentioned love either. Not really anyway.

Men were men, regardless of the species. But Gretchen was a hopeless romantic. Fuck, she wished it were true. Wished he could love her even a little bit. She turned her head so he wouldn't see her frown. Smiling at him when he took her hand.

The second he touched her, she pushed those negative thoughts aside. Whatever this was, and for however long it lasted, she was going to enjoy it.

Gretchen allowed Reg to steal her from her seat. She even giggled as his hands sought her skin beneath her shirt at her waist. He was extremely touchy feely, and she loved that about him. Loved it even more when he sat her down on his lap.

She was taller than him this way, and she liked having the advantage. Gretchen tugged his face up to hers, dropping long, tender kisses on his lips, then dipping her tongue inside his mouth.

An electrical sizzle of desire shot through her

whenever she was with him, and her panties were proof of that. Damn, he was perfect.

*Mine,* her Tiger growled possessively.

*Sheesh.*

She'd need to keep a lid on her beastie.

"Mmm, you taste good, *shona.* I wish I didn't have to return to the site we're working on. So, tell me how's work going today?"

She worked hard to rein in her inner slut, loving the hard feel of him beneath her ass, Knowing he wanted her just as much. The waiting would make later even better, and that was the only reason she was talking instead of ripping his clothes off.

"It's good. I just had the spunkiest grandma in the world as a client. She had me dye the tips of her hair pink."

"Cool. Doesn't sound like my grandma. She wore her hair in a braid and used to hit me and Robbie with wooden spoons when we were bad," he winked, and kissed her on her chin.

"Oh, yeah? I bet you deserved it." Gretchen giggled, picturing him as a kid when she realized what he'd said.

"Wait. Who?"

"Oh. My brother, Robbie."

"You have a brother?"

"Yep. He's a seal."

"He's not a Tiger?"

"Yes, he is a Tiger," he laughed, and she felt a warm blush spread over her cheeks.

"Rob is a Tiger Shifter, but he is also a Navy seal. We were both mischievous monsters when we were kids. Shifters have tons of energy, even if we can't always change into our animals till after puberty," he told her.

"Really? So, Elissa's not giving birth to an actual baby Tiger then?" she asked.

"No, just a baby, but we call our young *cubs*. He or she won't change until puberty, usually about thirteen or so," he shrugged nonchalantly, but his deep blue eyes landed on her stomach, and she could see the longing in them.

A child? Her body flushed with warmth, She had always wanted children, *er*, cubs.

It would be amazing, but not for a while yet, at least. She was no way near ready to have a baby. Besides, she'd been on birth control since she was a teen.

Reg had cured her fear about their lack of condom usage after explaining that Shifters don't typically get diseases, and they definitely did not get

STDs. She'd had a lot of questions, and he really did his best to answer them.

Sighing, Gretchen relaxed into Reg's arms, and he contented himself drawing little circles on her back. This was one of her favorite things about him.

*The cuddling.*

Her Reggie always seemed to want to hold her, and Gretchen was more than happy to comply. There hadn't been a lot of affection in her life growing up, and she relished each cuddle session for the gift it was.

He kissed her forehead and rested his cheek on top of her hair. He smelled so very good to her new supernaturally enhanced senses. Like fresh cut grass and a cool spring breeze.

Her inner she-Cat chuffed happily as she lay in his arms. She could definitely get used to this. That fact was worrisome in itself.

For weeks now, they had been inseparable. Either he'd spend the night at her place, or she'd go with him to his suite of rooms at the Pride House.

She'd been a little nervous at first. Being around Hunter and Elissa now that she knew who and what they were, basically her kickass bosses, was a little nerve wracking.

She might have had a little bitty bone to pick

with her best friend about the fact that she'd all but lied to her. A lie by omission was still a lie in her book. Gretchen had been pissed Elissa didn't tell her a thing about all this. Still was, a little.

*Imagine not explaining about Shifters to your own best friend! Hmph!*

The fact Shifters existed, and Elissa could now get all stripey and furry, were things she should have told her as her best friend. She could have shared *something,* for fuck's sake. At least, she should have in Gretchen's opinion.

The nerve of Elissa! It broke all the best friend rules, but it was water under the bridge now. She'd already forgiven Liss. And now, she understood the need for secrecy.

The supernatural world had to remain secret. It was vital to their survival, and very few humans were in the know. Gretchen couldn't even begin to grasp the many wonders and marvels that she had yet to discover.

That was all fine and good. Exciting even. There was just one thing that bothered her. Not knowing where she fit exactly. If only she could guarantee Reg would want her and be there with her for always.

*Sigh.*

Life didn't come with guarantees, so she'd have to

learn to enjoy this while she could. Her Tiger hissed and growled. The animal didn't like it when Gretchen's thoughts turned dark, but she couldn't help it.

Her future was tenuous at best. Hunter mentioned an induction ceremony into the Pride, but that was in passing. Reg seemed to like being with her, but he'd never said a thing about what came next for them.

*Hint hint.*

*How about something sparkly for that third finger on her left hand?*

Gretchen might be a Shifter now, but she'd been a human for thirty-years before that. She had very human expectations of how relationships progressed. There had been plenty of growling, kissing, tearing each other's clothes off, and hot, sweaty sex that ended in super amazing orgasms, and even biting, but she had yet to hear him say those oh so important three little words.

And yet, their absence hurt. Funny how three words could mean so much.

Why hadn't he said them? That was the thing truly driving her nuts. It was not like he was shy about anything else. Her sweet Reggie was always touching her and telling her she was beautiful.

She wasn't complaining, but she needed a little verbal affirmation. Maybe it was a Shifter thing. Maybe they were secret *commitment-phobes*.

Shifter society rules were out of her range of experience. Meeting the other Pride Mates had gone alright. The men were all sexy and huge, and the females gorgeous.

No one was as handsome as Reg, but still, they were a very good looking bunch. She had already met some of the women from the Pride.

They'd come to *Cut It Out* to either welcome her or just to look around her salon. Some of them, she hadn't recognized as Shifters since they'd visited before she went through the *Puspa*.

Others she'd met at the Pride House. In fact, one of them was her two o'clock. She glanced at the microwave and sighed.

"You have an appointment coming in, *shona*?"

"Yeah, a cut and blow dry at two with Pamela Brown, but I would rather stay here with you," she said regretfully.

"Pamela?"

"Yes, she's a Tiger from the Pride, right?" she asked missing the worried expression on his face.

"Yeah, she is. Be careful, okay? Pamela doesn't

play nicely with others. She can be a bit rude," he told her, frowning.

"Of course. Don't worry. I'm used to dealing with waspish females," she replied and smiled at him.

"Alright, well, I have to get going too. The crew is working on a repair to the exit ramp off I-95 to Barvale," Reg said, reaching for a kiss.

"You be careful too," she said.

"Uh huh," he nodded, and brushed her lips with his.

Shivers of anticipation made Gretchen tremble just before his lips, soft and firm, melded to hers. She swayed closer to him, loving the feel of all his rippling muscles against her softness.

There was just something about the man that knocked her completely off balance. Gretchen wiggled on his lap and felt the hard bar of his evident arousal beneath her ass. Desire flared between them, hot and quick as lightning, but the buzzing of the intercom broke them apart.

"That's Marion," she said, breathing heavy as Reg was.

"Later, we finish this later," he said firmly.

Dark blue eyes, like sapphires, held hers captive. Gretchen realized for the first time that the deep magical glow was his Tiger sneaking a peek at her.

She felt her own beast rush forward in response. The she-Tiger anxious to see her mate.

"Yes, later," she answered, despite all her reservations.

She was in too deep to deny him anything. Neither of them had made any declarations, but she knew exactly how she felt about him. Her own Tiger was more than thrilled by it, the damn beast was purring with emotion.

Gretchen was in love with the big, sexy man. She just didn't know if he loved her back.

*Grrrrr.*

Gretchen skipped into the salon tucking in her shirt and patting down her hair. That last goodbye kiss had left her a little disheveled. Smiling brightly, Gretchen turned to greet her two o'clock appointment.

The tall, skinny she-Tiger blinked slowly at Gretchen. She stared with hostility shining in her almond shaped eyes, glowing gold with her animal. Like Gretchen was so much dirt on her shoe. Tapping her red fingernails on her watch, she pursed her lips.

Gretchen glanced at the clock pointedly. It was two minutes after the hour. Not a big deal at all, but still, she was a professional, and it was her place of business. She plastered a smile on her face and apologized for her tardiness.

"Hi, you must be Pamela. Welcome to *Cut It Out*. I'm Gretchen---"

"You're late for my appointment," the she-Cat interrupted. "I hope you're better at cutting hair than you are at telling time."

"I do apologize. Why don't we get started? This way please," Gretchen waved her hand in the direction of the sinks and followed the woman as she walked over to the shampoo station.

Pamela Brown was a first-class beyotch, and Gretchen waited as the woman huffed out an annoyed breath and slunk down into the chair. It took two full pumps of shampoo, and three of conditioner to get the product out of the woman's over-processed locks.

So far, Gretchen had encountered several Shifters as clients, and they all had one thing in common. They were healthy AF, meaning their hair was often glossy and thick, and there was a shit ton of it.

But not hers. Pamela's hair, like her skin, seemed dull and gray. She was painfully thin, and that sullen, angry expression did nothing to enhance her looks or her attitude.

"I hate tardiness," Pamela bit out as she slunk into the seat at Gretchen's station.

"I am sorry," Gretchen replied through tight lips.

Her nose itched, and she wondered at the perfume the woman was wearing. Ever since she'd experienced the *Puspa*, Gretchen hadn't been able to wear any strong scents.

She'd attributed it to her brand new, extra-sensitive nose. But the female here was born a Shifter, and she was practically drowning in some cheap rose-scented fragrance.

It was cloying. Almost suffocating. Gretchen turned her head and sneezed into her elbow. Her body telling her to get away from the nasty woman.

"Oh, excuse me," she said, a little embarrassed.

"*Ohmygawd!* Let's just get on with this before I catch something," the she-Bitch muttered.

Gretchen bit her tongue. Marion was between clients at the moment, and he was watching the byplay without any amusement. It bolstered her confidence to know he was there and witnessing everything that was going on. She didn't need any nonsense cropping up because of this woman.

Some clients were just plain rude, she knew that having worked in this business over twelve years already. She shook her head at Marion before he could even think of interfering. It was good he was there, but she had this. Gretchen could handle herself just fine.

"Alright, so what did you have in mind for today?" Gretchen asked as she began running a comb through the woman's tangles as gently as possible. Not an easy feat.

*Holy flashback to 1984 and hairspray hell!*

The amount of product she'd washed out of Pamela's poor abused locks had been shocking, but that only eliminated half the problem with this woman's hair. Gretchen didn't know anyone who teased their hair anymore who was under sixty. Apparently, this woman didn't get the memo.

"Well, I need a trim obviously," she replied, that same waspish edge to her tone. "Then I'd like it blown out."

"Alright," Gretchen replied as pleasantly as possible and got to work.

The quicker she finished, the quicker the skinny woman could get the heck out of her store. Maybe she should start offering snacks while people waited?

In her opinion, hungry people were nasty people, and this woman was very thin. Not just thin, she looked emaciated, unhealthy, and her skin had a yellowish tint to it. Definitely not the way the Shifters Gretchen had already met looked.

*We can bite her in two*, her Tiger suggested.

Gretchen wanted to laugh but bit her tongue and tucked away the suggestion for later.

"Well, I'm surprised someone like you has managed to catch Reg's interest," Pamela remarked, fishing for gossip.

"Oh? What's that supposed to mean?"

"Nothing. I am just pointing out the obvious," she replied and eyed Gretchen's fuller frame as if that said everything.

"Ow!" shocked eyes looked up at Gretchen who shrugged.

"Sorry," she said, and didn't mean it. Gretchen had always been a no nonsense woman and she sure as fuck was not sugarcoating things for this mean-spirited woman. "Pamela, I have to be real here, you have a lot of knots, and some serious damage to your hair due to over-processing. If you want it to be healthy, I am going to have to take off more than a trim," Gretchen said.

"What? Are you sure?" Pamela asked, clearly shocked and worried. She looked at Gretchen warily. "You do have good hair," the woman said. "Okay, you can cut my hair, but before you do, look, I didn't mean anything by what I said. I just meant that you know how men are. They're all a bunch of players and Shifters are worse than humans."

For a moment, Pamela looked vulnerable and a little beaten, truth be told. As if life had been very hard on the female.

Gretchen still didn't exactly trust Pamela, but in the spirit of female solidarity, she felt herself softening towards her. The other she-Tiger was very pretty underneath all the paint and hair spray. Maybe she'd been used before. Maybe it left her angry and bitter.

It wasn't Gretchen's problem, but she could try and help. Too often did women pit themselves against other women. Gretchen was so over the whole *all women were in competition with each other* cliché.

She might not be ready to share her deepest fears with the woman, but she could help her with her hair for one thing. It wasn't all bad. Pamela simply used too many harsh products for her locks to be healthy.

In fact, everything about Pamela seemed overdone. Her makeup was thick and unflattering under the lights of the salon. It added a sharpness to her that was hard and cold, not very appealing to Gretchen.

"True, men can be pigs. But Reg is a good guy," Gretchen said.

Her Tiger hissed at the idea of anyone thinking or speaking badly about him. She soothed the beast by sticking up for him.

*Good mate.*

"Yeah, well, he certainly made his way through the Pride, breaking hearts. Even had a crush on Jessica before she hooked up with Brayden."

Gretchen's heart pounded inside her chest. Was that true? She'd come to think of Jessica as a friend, but the woman had never mentioned anything between her and Reg. Her Tiger snarled as anger and jealousy threatened to overwhelm her.

"Shifters are all the same. Love 'em and leave 'em, you know? Get a female to pop out a few cubs then it was out the door to thinner, younger pastures, if you catch my meaning," Pamela said, her eyes unfocused.

"Well, what about Elissa and Hunter?" Gretchen replied, clinging to the one couple she knew were inseparable.

"Oh, but that's different, isn't it? He is the Neta.

He needs his mate at his side to rule. Of course, he should have picked from his own Pride, but she went through the *Puspa,* so that part is fine for now. It's all in our laws, the ones the Shifter Council rules by," she told a wide eyed Gretchen, shrugging as if that explained everything.

"I suppose."

"The rest of these males are just a bunch of tomcats. Strutting around and sampling a new female every other month. Of course, for females it's different. We need a man during our heat to breed, but other than that we can do as we wish. Why, some females even share a male between them! It's not uncommon for either sex to have multiple partners."

"And what about mates?"

"Oh, well, when you're hooking up, you're considered mates, but nothing lasts forever, does it? Mates don't always work out…," she replied trailing off at the end.

Gretchen swallowed audibly at that little tidbit, missing the harsh expression on the other woman's face. She cut and styled Pamela's tawny-colored locks, pushing her thoughts aside and concentrating on her work. This was not the time nor the place.

There were too many people, and besides, she

shouldn't be having this talk with a stranger. So, Gretchen kept on working without missing a beat, losing herself in the familiarity of her chosen profession.

There was just something about hair that she loved. So many different colors, textures, and styles to work with. She sometimes felt like an artist, but instead of paints and brushes she used scissors and hair as her medium. Some of her up-do styles had even been featured in a few hair magazines and blogs.

Gretchen was more than content with her life's choices in so far as her career. Being a hair stylist was something she loved and excelled at. And now she was able to challenge herself even further by running her own salon. It was her dream come true. Professionally speaking.

Her personal life was another story. She'd expected to be married with kids by the time she'd hit thirty, but her last birthday had come and gone already. She'd never even had a serious boyfriend before.

Gretchen certainly enjoyed the opposite sex. The act itself had always been attractive to her, but she'd hardly had any success at it.

*Until Reg.*

The men she knew before him simply fell short of her expectations. The way things were going, she would have gladly considered Reggie her first real relationship. Him turning her into an actual furry and stripey Tiger wasn't something she'd expected.

Hell. She hadn't even known it was possible. She'd thought it made the two of them special, but maybe she'd been wrong. Maybe he was just another tomcat like Pamela said.

"All finished," Gretchen said quietly.

Her mood already deflated, Gretchen's heart was slowly breaking, and she wanted to throw her head back and yowl at the whole dang world. She looked at the woman in front of her without really seeing.

"Finally," the female murmured, crossing her arms over her chest.

Gretchen turned Pamela's chair around to face the mirror and waited blandly for her reaction. She had other things on her mind, and the way the woman received her new hairstyle was of little importance to her.

Though she did do a hell of a job cutting off the split ends and taming the unruly mess into a sleeker and more sophisticated cut that flattered her sharp features. Not that she deserved such treatment, Gretchen thought darkly.

The other she-Cat had spent thirty-minutes badmouthing the men of the Pride and dumping on every single hidden hope Gretchen had held for the future. Her head was positively spinning.

She might as well face the facts. Gretchen didn't know a damn thing about Shifters. Only bits and pieces she'd picked up here or there, tidbits dropped in passing by Reg, or Elissa, and now the bitchy Pamela. Couldn't someone just sit her down and tell her the whole damn truth of it all? She wanted to know everything. And she wanted to know now, dammit!

*Ugh.*

So far, the things she did know were not very promising. She'd told herself just that afternoon that things with Reg might not be permanent, but she sure did hope so. Only now, she wasn't so confident.

"It's a little short, but I guess it's okay." Pamela fingered her hair and squinted in the mirror. "Anyway, you just think about what I said. You might want to get out of Maverick Point while you can. Clingy exes just aren't attractive."

She dropped a fifty on the counter and walked

out. Considering the cut and dry was $48, the bitch had shorted Gretchen on the tip.

*Figured.*

Still, the skinny Tiger had done a number on her. She left Gretchen feeling all shook up inside and not in a good golden flow after sexy times way.

"Boss lady, I don't know what *Little Miss Thang* over there was whispering to you, but you should know she stood outside glaring at your man's car for like five-minutes before she stepped foot in here," Marion told her. His pink polished hands sat on his slim hips as he addressed Gretchen.

She could tell he was only getting started. Her new hire had decided off the bat that the two of them were going to be pals, and where Gretchen was very fond of the flashy, outspoken, and openly bisexual stylist, a scolding wasn't what she needed right now.

*Sigh.*

"So, what does that prove?" Gretchen returned distractedly.

"It proves you need to take what that skinny beyotch says with a grain of iodized salt, because I know she ain't kosher," he replied and narrowed his eyes.

"Marion!" Gretchen gasped and laughed. She

looked around to make sure the other clients were either distracted or busy.

"What? Think about it, Gretch. Clearly, she has an axe to grind, and it don't have nothing to do with you and your man. Listen sunshine, you can't let other people rain on your parade. Whatever she told you, talk to your man before you just go off and take it as gospel," he told her sagely, nodding his spikey head to emphasize his point.

"Thank you for your opinion, Mar. I appreciate you, but I need to work this out on my own."

Gretchen muddled through the rest of the day. Smiling took its toll, and by the time she closed the doors for the evening her face actually hurt. She felt emotionally raw and unsettled. It was a nasty, uneasy, grating feeling, but there was nothing she could do about it.

She needed to think. But she couldn't do that around Reg. When he was near there was only one thing she wanted, and it pained her to know she couldn't have it for keeps. She closed her eyes on a wave of sorrow and tried to keep her tears at bay.

*Him. I want him. Forever.*

*Mate,* her Tiger insisted, but Gretchen rejected the word.

According to Pamela it didn't mean anything special.

*Grrr,* her Tiger grumbled at the other woman's name, but again Gretchen ignored her beast.

She needed to call Reg to tell him to stay away, maybe then this feeling she had of being trapped in her own emotions would lessen.

She needed clarity, but she would only find that on her own.

# Chapter Twenty

Reg whistled as he made his way through the Pride House. Work had been a real bitch today. It seemed like Maverick Development was forever rebuilding roads and repairing exit ramps for the great state of New Jersey.

Not that he minded. He was good at his job. Now that Brayden was the foreman of his crew, things went a hell of a lot smoother for them.

Reg did not miss his ex-foreman and ex-Beta, Blake. Not one itty bitty bit.

That asshole had been the cause of so much misery and he'd almost cost the Nari her life. Reg was particularly fond of Elissa Maverick. She was the perfect mate for their fearless leader.

Shame filled him as he recalled his part in those

unfortunate turn of events. Luckily, the Neta had allowed Reg to tell his side of the story, and he'd been blessed with a second chance to prove himself to the Pride. They were the reason he felt worthy enough to remain in Maverick Point and to claim his fated mate. He owed a lot to Hunter and Elissa.

Ever since Rob had gone overseas, Reg had been responsible for taking care of himself. To his credit, Reg never gave up. Not even when he'd fucked up. Nope. He was not a quitter. Reg owned his fucking mistakes and learned from them.

And look how it paid off! He had his very own sweeter than honey fine as fuck mate waiting for him at the end of the day. He was one lucky moth-erfucker.

*Grrrrrr.*

Reg jumped in the shower and scrubbed off the dirt and grime of his day from his skin as quickly and thoroughly as he could. He wanted to hurry up and head over to Gretchen's place, but he insisted on being clean and fresh for her. She deserved him at his best.

*Always.*

His Tiger paced impatiently inside his mind's eye. The animal was always near to frenzying when-ever they were apart. He hated that she lived by herself. Wanted her with him, always, but she'd been human up until a few days ago.

He had to do things differently than he would have if she'd been born a Shifter. Differently was code for slowly.

But Reg was impatient. He tried to curb his eagerness, for her sake. Tonight he was going to broach the subject of living together. Fuck, he wanted that more than anything.

*"Give her some time to adjust, Reg,"* Mikey had told him.

The Pride healer was a little older, and presumably, wiser than Reg, what with his advanced education and all. So, he'd taken his advice gratefully, but he couldn't stop the creeping sensation that something was wrong. That he was fucking up by waiting.

*We are fated mates. Everything will be fine.*

Or so he'd told himself the last few days, but he did not know how much longer he could hold out. No. He was done sleeping apart. Tonight he would ask her to pick where she wanted to live. He didn't care where, as long as it was with her.

*Mine.*

Reg brushed his hair and donned a pair of soft faded jeans and a clean tee. It was sort of his uniform, he laughed at himself. Tonight was going to be special.

He had a surprise for his sweet Gretchen. Going slow was one thing, but he still needed her to know he was serious. Bite marks aside, he had a present for her, one she would hopefully understand and appreciate.

His cell phone rang as he pulled the pitcher of lemon infused water from the fridge to pour himself a glass. The sun was hot, in spite of the temperature capping at a brisk sixty-five degrees and Reg was parched.

He grinned and took a swig of the refreshing liquid. Ever since Hunter had mated Elissa, the Pride House had been stocked with all kinds of treats and goodies. Bowls filled to the brim with crushed red pepper kale chips and roasted dill chickpeas sat on the countertops for hungry Shifters. He nabbed a few and checked out who was calling him.

"Hey," he answered with a mouthful of the scrumptious snacks. "I was just about to leave---"

He was usually happy to hear from Gretchen, but his mate didn't sound all that happy to be calling. In fact, she sounded upset, and that made his Tiger all kinds of angry. The chickpeas turned to dust in his mouth when she told him the unthinkable.

"What are you talking about, Gretch?"

"I don't think we should see each other tonight, or maybe ever." she began.

"What? Why not?"

"I just need some space. You do too. We should think about things, you know?"

"No. I don't need to think anything over."

"Well, maybe I do. I mean, where is this going, anyway? I don't know anything about your lifestyle and I just, well, I just couldn't take it if you were just playing around with me, Reg. I think maybe it's better to end things now," she returned, her voice thick and shaky.

"I'm coming over," he replied and clicked the phone off before she could refuse him.

Reg was vibrating with fury. He looked down at the offensive, and broken, phone he'd crushed in his hand and chucked it across the room.

"Fuck!" he roared.

*She doesn't want to see me. Needs time to think. What did I do wrong?*

A million scenarios played through his mind. What could have happened?

He thought of the last time he'd seen her earlier that afternoon, and for the life of him, Reg couldn't recall a single thing he'd said or done to make his mate not want to see him.

"Reg?" Elissa padded into the room a look of concern on her face.

"Nari." Reg nodded out of respect for the Alpha female of the Pride. Her eyes were wide as she took in his angry stance and the broken cell phone.

"What did that phone ever do to you?" she asked and pointedly looked at the mess of broken glass and plastic marring the kitchen tile, then flicked her gaze back at him.

"Shit. Uh, I'm sorry," he grunted, and grabbed the broom and dustpan from the cabinet then proceeded to sweep up his mess. He knew Elissa would not go away without knowing what was going on.

He had to tell her what just happened, he thought and exhaled.

"That was Gretchen on the phone. She says she doesn't want to see me."

"Oh no! What happened?"

"I don't know, Nari. I saw her this afternoon and things were fine-"

"Something must have happened." Elissa pulled out a stool and sat down at the kitchen island and gestured for him to join her.

"Nothing, I swear. We ate, we kissed, we talked,

we hugged. She had an appointment with a client at two, and I had to go back to the road crew," he replied and clenched his fists. He tried his best to swallow the growl building up inside of him.

His Tiger was losing his shit, and this was no time to shift into his fur. The beast roared in his mind's eye, demanding he leave now and go hunt his mate.

*Find her, claim her again, make sure she knows who she belongs to.*

"Who was her two o'clock appointment with?"

"I don't know," he mumbled and ran his hands through his hair. Reg stopped. Fuck. He did know.

"Shit, *er*, I mean, *wait*. She had an appointment with Pamela at two."

"Pamela Brown? Yikes. Well, there's your problem," Elissa said.

She rolled her eyes at him, like it was fucking obvious, but Reg had no idea what she was talking about. As usual.

"With all due respect, Nari, what do you mean?"

"It means that skinny bitch Pamela got to our Gretchen. After that meeting you had with her and her pal out back, she was bound to make more trouble. Or don't you think I know what goes on in my own Pride?" Elissa growled with her hands on her protruding belly, looking for all the world like a fierce little mama Tiger.

Anger tore through him, and he'd never wanted to stalk and challenge a female so damn badly. Pamela and her friend were part of a group of she-Cats who'd messed around with Blake. They used to act all high and mighty because they were fucking the ex-Beta. Coming down a few pegs must have hurt their pride, so she'd gone after his mate.

*Big. Fucking. Mistake.*

"I said, what are you going to do about Gretchen, Reg?" Elissa interrupted his train of thought.

"Mine," he growled before he could stop himself. "Sorry, Liss," Reg looked at his Nari, and shrugged his shoulders.

"It's okay. I understand, but I've known Gretchen for a long time. I know she appears strong and confident, but she has the same misgivings and hang ups as the rest of the female population."

"Hang ups? About what?"

"A million things," she said. "Her hairstyle. Her weight. How she looks in a dress. You name it, all women get those same misgivings. We all feel like that sometimes---"

"Fuck tha- I mean, no. Unacceptable. She is my mate, Nari. She is perfect."

"I'm glad you think so, but have you told her that? Have you even told her what it means to be mates? I mean, you're still living here, Reg. It's been more than enough time to get acclimated to the situation, hasn't it? I would have gone mad without Hunter by my side for that long," Elissa told him bluntly.

"Fuck. I've messed up again, haven't I? All I wanted was to give her time to get used to the idea, and I wound up hurting her. I am such a fucking moron."

His heart pounded in his chest. Why couldn't he get this right? Well, he was a fuck up, but he could change. He would change. For her, he would do anything.

"Just a little hiccup, Reg, but you'll fix it. Now, go get her."

"Yes, Nari," he replied, and that was an order he didn't mind taking, for sure.

Reg was ready to go find his mate. He would hunt his *shona* down until he had her trapped in his arms where she belonged.

*Mine!*

# Chapter Twenty-One

Gretchen walked through the old church's lot until she reached the copse of fir trees that seemed to stand guard over the abandoned property.

She needed time away from Reg, and everyone else too. Time to just think.

Between that harpy yapping in her ear, Marion giving her the third degree, and her Tiger growling and hissing at her, she couldn't stand it another minute.

She'd locked up the salon after she tidied up and decided to go for a walk to clear her mind. First though, she'd had to have it out with Reg over the phone. That had not been fun.

What was she going to do about him? She ducked

behind a large shrub and began to remove her clothes. Her Tiger was pacing beneath her skin and wanted out. Gretchen understood the need.

Her she-Cat was strong and powerful, and a hell of a lot more certain of herself than Gretchen was. The animal hissed and spat at her human side for letting Pamela get to her.

She was Reg's fated mate and no matter what that woman said, she knew in her heart it meant more than just some sexy fun times between the sheets.

*Shit.*

She'd fucked up. She went and let that beyotch poison her mind. Gretchen hated it when she was wrong, but she was a big girl. She could admit it. And she was so very wrong. She owed Reg an apology.

"I'll do it, but first let's run off some of these feelings she-Cat. what do you say?" Gretchen asked her inner kitty in a soft whisper.

A breeze rustled the leaves in the tree above her, and within moments, she felt that familiar hum of magic wrap around her soft curves and brush against her skin. It was like stepping into a tub of warm water.

Slipping into her fur was getting easier, as she'd

been assured by her Shifter friends. The more frequently she did it, the more the pain diminished. After less than three minutes, she was shifted, taking a moment to adjust to her new shape.

She relished being in her new form. With her Tiger's eyes, she scoped out the landscape and sniffed the air. She was no expert, but she could tell she was alone, except for a family of rabbits hiding in a burrow beyond the pines. Her beast salivated for a moment, but Gretchen refused to indulge in a raw diet just yet.

Was she a bloodthirsty Shifter now? Maybe. But she was running this show whether her she-Cat liked it or not and Gretchen put her foot down when it came to eating cute, cotton-tailed bunnies.

*Grrr.*

*Ew. No.*

The woods stretched for miles and miles over Burlington County, and she was anxious to get some of that open space under her claws. She'd already explored some of it with Reg by her side.

Christ, she missed him! Wished he was there, even though she'd been the one who'd ordered him to stay away. The man had always been so sweet with her and patient.

Truthfully, staying away from him hurt her more

than he ever had. Gretchen wanted to be with him all the time. He was constantly on her mind, in her heart, stamped on her skin, like her tattooed Tiger. She chuffed and ran harder.

*That is because he is our mate,* her Tiger voiced her opinion in her mind, but it did not fill her with any kind of ease.

Yes, he was her mate. But what did that mean to him? She felt foolish and a little needy, but fucking hell, what did a girl have to do to get a man to declare his feelings and intentions already?

The time she'd asked him for was not for her. It was for him. So, he could figure out how he felt. She knew how she felt already.

Gretchen was in love with him. She'd already admitted it, *well,* to herself anyway. Not a half-assed love either. This was the once in a lifetime, shooting star, all-encompassing tsunami kind of love that made her heart pound and her pulse race. She'd never felt it before, but she felt it now. For Reg.

She stopped running as she came upon a group of rocks and what looked like the mouth of a cave. There was a small stream nearby and, *sniff,* was that urine?

Gretchen hissed and swatted her nose. It was as if someone had marked the territory in the most animalistic way. By letting loose with his groove thing and spraying the fuck out of the wooded area with his strong pneumonia-like urine.

*Ew. So fucking gross.*

Gretchen heard someone coming. Her Tiger crouched, unable to determine the scents she was getting through all that stinky piss smell. She growled when two figures emerged.

"What have we here?" the male said.

Gretchen hissed and spat at him, turning to the female who was familiar. Fuck. Was that Pamela?

"You should have gone after I warned you about what the males here were like. I tried to give you a heads up," Pamela said in a small voice.

She looked so skinny and fragile, bruised too, and Gretchen turned to the male and hissed at him. Those marks on her were fresh, and the fear in her eyes had been placed there by him, she was sure.

"Well, well, looks like we have another Pride bitch who needs to get mounted to learn her place," the unfamiliar male growled.

"Leave her alone, Carl," Pamela said, moving in front of her.

The male growled, his blood stained his lips turning down as he raised an arm and struck Pamela viciously with his fist right in her stomach. She buckled over, and Gretchen snarled, standing in front of the woman. Pamela was gasping in pain. She might not have been the friendliest person to Gretchen, but she did not deserve this treatment.

No one did.

"Come on, whore. I'll show you what you're good for," the angry male said, a strange, high-pitched laughing escaping his lips.

Gretchen backed up, using her furry butt to try to push Pamela back into the tree line. The woman was still struggling to breathe, but she understood, and she was crawling on her hands and knees.

Gretchen spared her a glance, angry at the dozen or more bite marks and scratches she saw marring her skin. Some were old, others new. This was systematic abuse, she thought angrily.

The male approached, and she recognized something off about his smell. She didn't understand it, but she knew he wasn't a Tiger. It was something else. He threw his head back and cackled again. That was when it hit her. His scent was different because he was not a Tiger or Bear, like the Shifters she had encountered. He was something else. Something she recognized from countless hours watching the animal channel.

*Hyena,* her Tiger spat the word.

"No," Pamela stood up, turning to Gretchen, and mouthing the word run, before she ran at the male.

He turned on her, smacking the skinny woman down with a hard fist. Pamela crumbled to the floor unconscious before Gretchen could even react. The bastard had struck the woman without any warning.

"Come on, bitch, I'll show you what a real man does to a pussy," he snarled, and began to stalk her.

Gretchen didn't know much, but she was bigger than the stranger. At least, she was while in her fur, anyway. She just couldn't let him change.

Taking a chance, she moved forward, swiping at him with her extended claw. Her plan of attack was thwarted when the bastard revealed a whip hidden in his right hand.

The long metal weapon flew out and the clawed tip caught her on the shoulder. He yanked it back, tearing at her flesh, and Gretchen roared in outrage. The fucker had ripped a chunk of her hide clean off.

Fury enveloped her, and she growled and snarled as her copper-scented blood filled the air. Just as she was about to try for the man again, an ear-splitting roar filled her ears.

"Another fucking cat? Oh, you think your hero will save you? Let's see how he does against me," the

Hyena cackled, and snapped the metal whip towards Reg who had just arrived.

Gretchen's heart leapt in her throat as her mate charged. Reg roared, moving quick as lightning across the clearing. He dodged past the boulders that sat on the left of the cave were Pamela and the Hyena had been having they're whatever the fuck it was.

That bastard unleashed his whip catching Reg in his side, but before Gretchen could react her mate went from standing on four feet to two. Then Gretchen saw something she'd never thought possible.

It was as if Reg was somehow able to keep part of his Tiger form, shifting only his hands to human. With his opposable thumbs he was able to grip the end of the whip, wrapping it around his forearm and engaging in a very uneven tug-of-war with the Hyena.

Gretchen couldn't move. She was frozen like a deer in headlights. Well, almost. She noticed Pamela stirring and ran over to the woman, never taking her eyes off her mate. As Reg pulled, the Hyena Shifter was forced closer and closer to his deadly jaws.

The man yelled and Gretchen swore he begged as he was dragged closer to those mighty teeth. Her

Tiger stilled, watching approvingly as her mate defended her. But the human side of Gretchen couldn't help but cry out as she switched fur for skin.

"Reg!" she yelled.

He turned his glowing sapphire gaze on her, and he stopped before he could close his jaws over the man's throat. Last second, Reg clocked him with a wicked left hook and wrapped the man's own steel whip around the bastard.

He tied him up and dropped him before completing his transformation to human. Gretchen gasped and grateful tears fell from her eyes as Reg ran to her.

He scooped her up in his arms checking her for injury. She clung to him, breathing heavily. Her wound burned but was already closing. Rapid healing being one of the perks of her new furry abilities.

"*Shona*, are you okay? Did he hurt you anywhere else?"

Pamela stirred, and Reg roared aloud. The woman whimpered and kept her eyes on the floor.

"It's not her fault, he hurt her too." Gretchen explained, standing up for a whimpering Pamela.

"Sorry," he growled, his blue eyes searching over her.

"Reg, I am so sorry, I didn't mean to run into them. They were just here," she explained, but he just held her tighter, pressing his head to her neck.

"It's okay. Find her phone and call Elissa. Tell Hunter where we are while I make sure that bastard doesn't try anything."

Gretchen nodded, turning to Pamela who was searching through her discarded clothing with trembling hands. She handed her a cell phone and Gretchen dialed, encouraging her to dress.

Turning around, she watched in awe as Reg took command of the situation. There was something intensely hot about a strong male that had both her human and her Tiger halves growling in approval.

Reg made sure the Hyena Shifter was secured while they waited for the Pride Neta, and the rest of the guard to come to the clearing. Luckily, Elissa and Hunter arrived first, bringing them spare sweats and socks.

The natural born Shifters might be comfortable walking around naked, but Elissa wasn't. She ignored the Nari's giggles when she found Gretchen hiding behind a tree.

Reg had simply smiled and blocked Gretchen

with his own body as he took the clothes from Elissa. Of course, that meant he was standing there with that lengthy lead pipe he called a cock just waving in the wind in front of another woman!

*Grrrrr.*

"Hey," Gretchen growled and jumped in front of her mate. Which made him growl when Hunter walked into their line of vision.

"Okay, you two, stop growling! Get dressed so we can handle this shit show," he bellowed.

Both Gretchen and Reg stilled at their Neta's shouted command. Against the tree with her mate beside her she felt a little trapped, but she'd never been so happy in all her life.

*"Shona?"*

"We'll talk, Reg, as soon as we are alone," She promised him.

It took a little more than an hour to collect evidence from the scene and secure the Hyena to be brought towards the Shifter Council for trial. Pamela did not hesitate to confess to Hunter what had been going on.

Gretchen listened, sitting beside Elissa who was crying at the words that flowed from the poor battered female. It seemed Blake had been pimping out the females of the Pride to other local Shifter groups to garner favor.

Naturally, the forced prostitution had made females, like Pamela, distrustful of the males of the Pride, and catty to the females whom they believed allowed and even encouraged the practice.

Of course, they couldn't have been more wrong. Hunter had roared and snarled in outrage. Elissa had quieted the male, taking Pamela into her arms. She rocked the woman, promising her that she and the other women would be seen by the doctor of their choice, taken to counseling, and that they would all be welcomed into the Pride House until they felt safe and protected.

Elissa asked for one thing in return. The females needed to help her by creating a list of the names of the Shifters who had participated in this atrocity. The list would be presented to the Council so the guilty could be tried for their crimes.

"Really? You would do that?" Pamela had asked, her eyes full of hope and disbelief.

"You're damn fucking straight," Elissa replied, taking the woman's hand in hers.

"And I will help," Gretchen added.

She had swallowed her own tears at hearing just the periphery of Pamela's tale and could not imagine the horrors that would be revealed when more of the females came forward. This was going to be painful, but if the Maverick Pride was as strong as Reg said it was, then they could handle it. Together.

Gretchen was glad when they were finally permitted to leave. The events that had unfolded had been harrowing and scary. All she wanted was a hot bath and her mate.

*Mate,* her Tiger seconded.

"You ready to go, *shona*? I think we need to talk."

"I'm ready, Reg," she replied, knowing the best was yet to come.

Her mate had come after her when she'd turned him away. He had rescued her from the clutches of that warped Hyena, and though, he had probably wanted to rip the guy's head off, he had deferred to her still human sensibilities, and merely immobilized him.

He might not have said it yet, but Reg cared about her. She knew he did. It was time to stop being a coward. There was no written rule anywhere that said a man had to be the first to confess his love.

Gretchen was a modern woman. She was in love for the first, and last, time of her life. Now, she just had to tell him. Her tiger chuffed and purred at the thought, the beast anxious to get him home, naked, and in her bed.

What better place for her to make her not so secret confession?

*Prrrrrrrrrrr.*

# Epilogue

Reg turned Gretchen under the spray of warm water to rinse the shampoo from her hair. He'd insisted on getting her undressed and into the shower as soon as they'd finished explaining the situation to Hunter.

"I can't believe you got this done today," she said, running her hands over his already healed chest in awe.

It was the surprise he'd gotten for her. A way for her to understand where she belonged in his life. He was so fucking happy she liked it.

Directly over his heart and spanning most of the left side of his body, Reg now sported an intricate, and magically crafted, tattoo that he'd gotten specifically for his mate.

He had spent over an hour being tattooed by a very efficient, semi-sadistic Witch who used magic to wield his ink gun at ten times the regular speed.

The image was of two Bengal Tigers representing Reg and his *shona*, side by side. One had a very easily identifiable tuft of white fur on the tip of her tail with baby blue eyes. She was the prettiest damn thing he'd ever seen.

The male Tiger was larger, and his eyes were focused on his female. They were a darker blue color, like his own. The male cradled his mate from behind wrapping his tale protectively around her.

Tiger blossoms drifted down from above them with a whisper of Mount Maverick rising behind them. The flowers were a reminder of her beautiful scent, and the entire image was a tribute to his undying love for her.

*His fated mate. His one and only.*

Reg only hoped she understood.

"How come it's healed already?"

"The same reason your shoulder is healed. We are Shifters, *shona*. We heal quickly. Our magic allows that. Do you like it?"

"It's beautiful," she said.

The tiny movements of her hand on his chest were creating a not so tiny reaction below his belly button, but he ignored his erection for now. She already knew his body worshipped her, but he needed her to understand his heart did too.

"You're so beautiful, Gretchen. Everything I ever wanted, and I know you deserve better, but I can't let you go," he told her.

His voice sounded like he'd swallowed gravel, but his beast was pushing him hard. He was satisfied she was whole and unhurt, and fuck yeah, he was desperate to enjoy more carnal delights. But he needed to get this out first.

"Oh Reg---"

"Let me finish, my beautiful *shona*," he started.

He watched her blush spread across her cheeks and down to her beautifully ripe breasts. Further still, his gaze dropped to the close crop curls that hid her from view.

"Fuck, you smell good," he murmured, as the scent of her arousal reached his nostrils. Reg growled, shutting off the water and grabbing a pair of towels for them.

he wrapped the soft bath sheet around her body and lifted her up in his arms like the treasure she was. He wanted her more than anything, but first they needed to clear the air.

"Need you, Reg," she said, and lifted her face to his lips.

He kissed her readily and pressed his forehead to hers. His dick throbbed painfully, but he held himself in check. There was nothing he desired more than to sink into his mate's heat. Nothing except maybe sinking deep into her heart as well.

Reg could kiss her and forget all their problems for the moment, but they would still exist like a wall between them. No way, he outright refused to be separated from her in any way.

Something had sent her running from him earlier that afternoon. Something that Pamela had said or done. It should not have affected his mate so, but it did. So much so that she told him to stay away again. The pain was still fresh, and it hurt to even think about leaving her.

He needed to figure out what had happened. What the other Tiger had said to his feisty mate that made her doubt him. The only way to learn the truth, was to simply ask her. Sucking up his courage, Reg proceeded to do just that.

"Why did you tell me to stay away from you today, shona? What did I do wrong?" he asked with a sadness he couldn't help creeping into his voice.

He sat down on the bed with her on his lap and watched her expression change from lustful to thoughtful. Tears welled in her eyes, and she bit her lip. He hated to see her look so upset, but then she straightened her shoulders and looked at him through her glassy baby blues.

"I suppose I owe you an explanation."

"You don't owe me anything, I just want to fix this. I need to make this right because I can't be away from you another night. I need you with me here, now, always, You are my fated mate, Gretchen. You're a part of my soul. How can I be expected to live without the other half of myself?"

"Why didn't you say this before?"

"I am so sorry, shona. I should have," he said. "I told you, I'm not good with words, but if you need them, I will try."

Then he looked into her big eyes, cupping her face with his hands, brushing away her tears. He didn't deserve her, but he would spend every fucking day trying to. He vowed to do anything he had to, to make sure she never cried again.

"I love you, *shona.* Since the day I saw you, I have loved you and only you. I will do anything, baby. Tell me what I need to do to make this right," Reg said, his expression shocked as Gretchen gasped and began to sob openly.

"Gretchen? Shona!"

Before he could say anything else, his mate stood up, and he was about to follow her when she turned. Her eyes glowed before she moved, and admittedly, Reg wasn't prepared for her to tackle him.

But she did, thank fuck, and they almost wound up on the floor. His quick reflexes saved them both, but before he could speak, she was kissing him.

*Fuck*, was she kissing him.! He groaned and moaned into her mouth, desperate for her. But before things could get out of control, she pulled back.

"Oh Reg, I was so confused. I didn't understand what fated mates meant, and Pamela got in my head, talking about what players you Shifters are. Now I know why she feels that way, but I'm so sorry. I should have come to you first. I'd actually decided to call you when I went out for a run. I just wanted some air, but then I ran into them, and you know the rest," she finished and wrapped her arms around his neck, holding him tightly to her.

"You could have been hurt," he growled, and tried to sound angry, but his body was already reacting predictably to her nearness.

"But I wasn't. You saved me."

"Love you, mate. Only you. So much."

"I know. I love you too," she answered, and stroked his chest down his abdomen to where he wanted her the most. "If I didn't realize it before that beautiful tattoo would have shown me. Let's not let anything come between us again, okay?"

"Never," he vowed. "I want you for always, Gretchen. As my mate, as my partner, as part of my Pride, and as my wife. Will you marry me, *shona?*"

"What? Really? Yes, oh yes, I will," she shouted and mashed her lips to his.

Reg rolled them around the bed, kissing the fuck out of her. He did not stop until he was where he wanted to be, directly beneath her supple curves. He tugged the towel, and then nothing stood between them.

*No walls. No misunderstandings. Only love.*

"You know, when I first met you, I knew you were my mate. There is something inside of us Shifters that alerts us when we've met our fated mates."

"Is that so?"

"Yes. I wanted you so desperately, I came up with a plan. I was going to set a trap, I was gonna be the most dedicated boyfriend you ever saw so that you would fall for me. Then I was gonna tell you about Shifters, claim you as mine."

"Yeah? Then what happened?" she purred and opened her legs wide.

Her slick folds caressed his hardened length, and Reg almost lost his train of thought. Up and down, she moved and glided, teasing them both into a frenzy.

"Well, I got it wrong, *shona*," he grunted as she kissed the head of his swollen cock with her wet slit, sliding just the tip in and out of her heat so fucking slowly he went cross-eyed.

"How's that?"

"I didn't trap you," he groaned, and she pressed down on him, sucking him inside her heated core one inch at a time. "Fuck, *shona*, feels s'good."

"You didn't trap me?" she moaned, and flexed her hips, swallowing him deeper still.

"Nope. You're the one who's got me *purrfectly trapped*, and I never want you to let me go."

"Never. Mine," she growled.

Then she began to move, slowly, seductively, and certainly. Just enough to drive him completely out of his mind. His sweet Gretchen pressed down on his chest and abdomen, using his muscles to hold herself as she rocked her body back and forth. So breathtakingly beautiful, panting and moaning. So responsive.

She rode him harder and faster. Making him grunt and pant and moan with every move. So attuned to his wants and needs she worked him until Reg saw stars explode behind his eyes.

"Need you to come for me, *shona*," he sat up, taking control of her thrusts.

Reg grabbed hold of his luscious mate's hips and lifted her up and down. He loved watching her face, the expression of pure bliss as her head fell back, and she moaned his name. Reg caught her nipple in his mouth and her eyes rolled back in ecstasy. He thrusted upwards, using all his strength and skill.

Gretchen cried out, scratching his shoulders like the wild cat she was. Her pussy gripped him, squeezing his cock as she fell into orgasm.

"Come with me, Reg," she begged.

How could he resist an offer like that? Reg thrust upwards, once, twice, he lifted her and slammed her down, grinding her on his cock until he joined her. Incandescent lights exploded behind his eyes.

Together they rocketed and spiraled out beyond their bedroom. Past Maverick Point, past the Earth, into outer space and beyond. Entire universes were destroyed and created in the strength of their climax and solidifying of their mate bond.

Where it was thin and silvery before, Reg saw a solid platinum ethereal link between him and his mate in that other plane of reality where their beasts rested together until called. He blinked as he fell slowly back to earth, cradling his mate on top of him. He stroked her hair and her neck too tired to do anything else.

"Reg?"

"Mm?"

"Let's do that again," she sat up and grinned, and suddenly, Reg wasn't tired at all. He would never be tired as long as Gretchen wanted him.

"I love you, *shona*," he said, and he meant it all the way to the depths of his soul.

"Show me."

His sweet little mate bit her lip expectantly, and Reg did not disappoint her. He would spend eternity trying to be the mate she deserved. Gretchen was not worried about it, and she told him often. He was the only male for her, something that had him strutting more often than not.

*Together, they were purrfect.*

· · ·

The end.

Did you enjoy this story? Check out the rest of the Maverick Pride Tales today!

# P.S

Don't forget to tell me how you liked this story by leaving your honest review!

*No pressure.* 😉

A review can be one or two brief sentences where you simply state whether you enjoyed the story and would recommend it to someone! It is an enormous help to authors and the best way for us to reach larger audiences so we can keep writing the stories you love!

Thank you so much!

Xoxo!

Del mare alla stella,

C.D. Gorri

# *Have you met my Bears?*

Looking for a Paranormal Romance series that is loads of growly fun?

Meet the Barvale Clan first in the Bear Claw Tales! A complete shifter romance series about 4 brothers who discover and need to win their fated mates!

Followed by two more spin off series, the Barvale Clan Tales and the Barvale Holiday Tales!

No cliffhangers. Steamy PNR fun.
Go and read your next happily ever after today!

# Beware... Here Be Dragons!

The Falk Clan Tales began as my stories surrounding four dragon Brothers and how they find their one true mates, but when a long lost brother arrives on the scene, followed by a few more Shifters…what can I say? The more the merrier!

Each Dragon's chest is marked with his rose, the magical link to his heart and his magic. They each have a matching gemstone to go with it.

**She's given up on love, but he's just begun.**

In *The Dragon's Valentine* we meet the eldest Falk brother, Callius. He is on a mission to find a Castle and his one true mate, one he can trust with his diamond rose....

**His heart is frozen; can she change his mind about love?**

In *The Dragon's Christmas Gift* our attention shifts to Alexsander, the youngest brother of the four. He has resigned himself to a life alone, until he meets *her*.

**Some wounds run deep, can a Dragon's heart be unbroken?**

*The Dragon's Heart* is the story of Edric Falk who has vowed never to love again, but that changes when he meets his feisty mate, Joselyn Curacao.

**She just wants a little fun, he's looking for a lifetime.**

We finally meet Nikolai Falk and his sexy Shifter mate in *The Dragon's Secret*.

*Now available in a boxed set.*

Guess what…. I've got more Dragons on the way!

Look for The Dragon's Treasure now available, and the upcoming The Dragon's Dream and The Dragon's Surprise!

## Other Titles by C.D. Gorri

### Young Adult Urban Fantasy Books:

Wolf Moon: A Grazi Kelly Novel Book 1

Hunter Moon: A Grazi Kelly Novel Book 2

Rebel Moon: A Grazi Kelly Novel Book 3

Winter Moon: A Grazi Kelly Novel Book 4

Chasing The Moon: A Grazi Kelly Short 5

Blood Moon: A Grazi Kelly Novel 6

*Get all 6 books NOW AVAILABLE IN A BOXED SET:

The Complete Grazi Kelly Novel Series

Casting Magic: The Angela Tanner Files 1

Keeping Magic: The Angela Tanner Files 2

### G'Witches Magical Mysteries Series

Co-written with P. Mattern

G'Witches

G'Witches 2: The Hary Harbinger

Paranormal Romance Books:

Macconwood Pack Novel Series:

Charley's Christmas Wolf: A Macconwood Pack Novel 1

Cat's Howl: A Macconwood Pack Novel 2

Code Wolf: A Macconwood Pack Novel 3

The Witch and The Werewolf: A Macconwood Pack Novel 4

To Claim a Wolf: A Macconwood Pack Novel 5

Conall's Mate: A Macconwood Pack Novel 6

Her Solstice Wolf: A Macconwood Pack Novel 7

Werewolf Fever: A Macconwood Pack Novel 8

Also available in 2 boxed sets:

The Macconwood Pack Volume 1

The Macconwood Pack Volume 2

Macconwood Pack Tales Series:

Wolf Bride: The Story of Ailis and Eoghan A Macconwood Pack Tale 1

Summer Bite: A Macconwood Pack Tale 2

His Winter Mate: A Macconwood Pack Tale 3

Snow Angel: A Macconwood Pack Tale 4

Charley's Baby Surprise: A Macconwood Pack Tale 5

Home for the Howlidays: A Macconwood Pack Tale 6

A Silver Wedding: A Macconwood Pack Tale 7

Mine Furever: A Macconwood Pack Tale 8

A Furry Little Christmas: A Macconwood Pack Tale 9

Also available in two boxed sets:

The Macconwood Pack Tales Volume 1

Shifters Furever: The Macconwood Pack Tales Volume 2

<u>The Falk Clan Tales:</u>

The Dragon's Valentine: A Falk Clan Novel 1

The Dragon's Christmas Gift: A Falk Clan Novel 2

The Dragon's Heart: A Falk Clan Novel 3

The Dragon's Secret: A Falk Clan Novel 4

The Dragon's Treasure: A Falk Clan Novel 5

Dragon Mates: The Falk Clan Series Boxed Set Books 1-4

<u>The Bear Claw Tales:</u>

Bearly Breathing: A Bear Claw Tale 1

Bearly There: A Bear Claw Tale 2

Bearly Tamed: A Bear Claw Tale 3

Bearly Mated: A Bear Claw Tale 4

Also available in a boxed set:

The Complete Bear Claw Tales (Books 1-4)

<u>The Barvale Clan Tales:</u>

Polar Opposites: The Barvale Clan Tales 1

Polar Outbreak: The Barvale Clan Tales 2

Polar Compound: A Barvale Clan Tale 3

Polar Curve: A Barvale Clan Tale 4

Also available in a boxed set:

The Barvale Clan Tales (Books 1-4)

<u>Barvale Holiday Tales:</u>

A Bear For Christmas

Hers To Bear

Thank You Beary Much

Also available in a boxed set:

The Barvale Holiday Tales (Books 1-3)

<u>Purely Paranormal Romance Books:</u>

Marked by the Devil: Purely Paranormal Romance Books

Mated to the Dragon King: Purely Paranormal Romance Books

Claimed by the Demon: Purely Paranormal Romance Books

Christmas with a Devil, a Dragon King, & a Demon: Purely Paranormal Romance Books

Vampire Lover: Purely Paranormal Romance Books

Grizzly Lover: Purely Paranormal Romance Books

Elvish Lover: Purely Paranormal Romance Books

Hot Dire Wolf Nights: Purely Paranormal Romance

Books

Christmas With Her Chupacabra: Purely Paranormal Romance Books

The Wardens of Terra:

Bound by Air: The Wardens of Terra Book 1

Star Kissed: A Wardens of Terra Short

Waterlocked: The Wardens of Terra Book 2

Moon Kissed: A Wardens of Terra Short

*Now in a boxed set and in audio!

The Maverick Pride Tales:

Purrfectly Mated

Purrfectly Kissed

Purrfectly Trapped

& More coming

Dire Wolf Mates:

SERIES MAKEOVER COMING SOON

Wyvern Protection Unit:

SERIES MAKEOVER COMING SOON

Standalones:

The Enforcer

Blood Song: A Sanguinem Council Book

EveL Worlds:

Chinchilla and the Devil: A FUCN'A Book

Sammi and the Jersey Bull: A FUCN'A Book

Mouse and the Ball: A FUCN'A Book

The Guardians of Chaos:

Wolf Shield: Guardians of Chaos Book1

Dragon Shield: Guardians of Chaos Book 2

Stallion Shield: Guardians of Chaos Book 3

Panther Shield: Guardians of Chaos 4

Witch Shield: Guardians of Chaos 5

Howl's Romance

Mated to the Werewolf Next Door: A Howl's Romance

The Tiger King's Christmas Bride

Claiming His Virgin Mate: Howls Romance

Twice Mated Tales

Doubly Claimed

Doubly Bound

Doubly Tied

Hearts of Stone Series

Shifter Mountain: Hearts of Stone 1

Shifter City: Hearts of Stone 2

Shifter Village: Hearts of Stone 3

Accidentally Undead Series

Fangs For Nothin'

Moongate Island Tales

Moongate Island Mate

Mated in Hope Falls

Mated by Moonlight

Speed Dating with the Denizens of the Underworld

Ash: Speed Dating with the Denizens of Underworld

Arachne: Speed Dating with the Denizens of Underworld

Hungry Fur Love

Hungry Like Her Wolf: Magic and Mayhem Universe

Hungry For Her Bear: Magic and Mayhem Universe

Shifters Unleashed Boxed Sets

Check out these amazing anthologies where you can find some of my books and the works of other awesome authors!

Midnight Magic Anthology (Water Witch)

Rituals & Runes Anthology (Air Witch)

Island Stripe Pride

Tiger Claimed

Tiger Denied

NYC Shifter Tales

Cuff Linked

Sealed Fate

A Howlin' Good Fairytale Retelling

Sweet As Candy (as seen in Once Upon An Ever After)

Shelly Maypo Mysteries

Spring Fling (co-written with P. Mattern)


<u>Coming Soon:</u>

If The Shoe Fits: A Howlin' Good Fairytale Retelling

For Fangs Sake

Moongate Island Captive

The Dragon's Surprise

The Dragon's Dream

Bearing Gifts

Taming Magic: The Angela Tanner Files 3

Vampire Shield: Guardians of Chaos 6

Chickee and the Paparazzi: FUCN'A

The Wolf's Winter Wish: A Macconwood Pack Tale

The Hybrid Assassin

Tiger Rejected

# Excerpt from Wolf Shield: Guardians of Chaos

What a day! Fergie McAndrews headed towards the pick-up truck she'd borrowed from her roommate for work that morning.

Of course, the thirty-thousand dollar certified used luxury car she'd splurged on earlier in the year was in the shop. Again.

Just another in a long line of bad decisions. After leaving a perfectly good job for a startup company, she was laid off three weeks ago and had to borrow money from her parents to pay rent. Wasn't that humiliating?

*"This is the last time, Ferg," her step-monster had said after she'd Venmo'd the money to her.*

God forbid the mechanic call and tell her the car

was ready. She wouldn't be able to pick it up for another week. That was when she got her first paycheck from her newest gig at L-Corp. Not a startup, but an older company with new offices in Bayonne, which was only a half-hour commute.

But to commute, you needed a car. Fergie had no choice but to borrow the old pick-up from her best friend and roommate, Jessenia Banks. It wasn't like she needed the truck. She worked from home these days. Besides, Fergie promised to fill it up and have it washed.

She huffed out a breath. It'd been a really long day. A crappy one too. Fergie wanted to love her new job. Really, she did. But so far, it was the pits. If Fergie wanted to be a librarian, she would've been one.

Research was her jam. Well, when it was interesting. She had a knack for sniffing out information and compiling easy-to-read spreadsheets and time-lines. It wasn't the hard work that annoyed her. Her complaint was the content. The actual stuff her new boss had her looking up. It was beyond boring.

Why an enormous conglomerate like L-Corp needed old land surveys, cross-referenced with newspaper reports on accidents, crimes, etcetera.

She had no idea. She'd been at it for weeks now. So far, she'd researched six locations given via GPS coordinates across Hudson County. Her new boss wanted everything, every little insignificant piece of information she could dig up.

That was the easy part. It was the hassle of the actual job that really made her want to give up. Every day she had to drive to Bayonne to pick up her work laptop she'd dropped off the night before with all of that day's findings. Every single night they wiped her computer clean.

Like she was going to run away with the secrets of what happened on 2$^{nd}$ and Washington sixty-years ago. Can you say paranoid? Ugh.

Fergie had always looked forward to working for a huge global company. It was supposed to be her ticket out of the Garden State. Traveling the globe, seeing new things, visiting far-off places was always a secret dream of hers. Well, that, and having her own walk-in closet full of gorgeous designer shoes.

*Best secret dream evah!* In her opinion, anyway. What woman didn't love shoes? Fergie hummed as she daydreamed about rows and rows of Blahnik's, Jimmy Choo's, Garavani's, Ferragamo's, and her personal favorites, Louboutin's on every shelf!

Don't judge. Fergie wasn't shallow, she just liked pretty things. Haters gonna hate. But every time she ran across a thrift or second-chance store, she'd search high and low to see what they had. That was how she'd scored the pumps on her feet.

They made her feel good about herself. Being five-foot two-inches short with more curves than a racetrack, Fergie had had more than her fair share of self-esteem issues growing up. Alright, so she was chubby. She could admit that proudly now.

If everyone looked the same, the world would be one boring as hell place. Fergie liked herself perfectly fine these days, in spite of all the times her step-monster tried to make her diet growing up. So she liked food and shoes. Big deal.

She worked hard to feed and clothe herself, so as far as she was concerned, no one had a right to comment. So what if she wanted some excitement in her life? Fergie was aware she was better off than most, but what was wrong with having goals?

She'd spent a lot of time thinking about how a woman like her could have an adventure. Travelling was the only thing she could think of. Of course, she'd been hoping this job would be the answer to that. Even travelling for work was better than being stuck.

*Sigh.*

So far, her plans had fallen flat, but hey, at least she was earning a paycheck. Her new boss, Mr. Offner, might be a strange man, but he signed her checks, and that was enough for now. Fergie had never seen more than a glimpse of him. All of her instructions usually came via email.

Most of the time she was able to compile her research quickly, then she'd head back to the office to organize it into neat little spreadsheets, and finally, she'd hand it all in with her laptop. But not today.

Mr. Offner sent her an email detailing everything she could dig up on one of the oldest places on record in the county. Of course, land surveys that old, along with police reports, newspaper articles, deeds, and sales records were nowhere she could easily access them.

After wasting hours at both the court house and municipal building, Fergie had been directed to the *second* public library. Apparently anything over a hundred years old was filed away in the godforsaken place. She'd been shocked to find an entire room filled with musty old archives. And wouldn't you know it, there was no cell service and no internet access. Plus, their phone lines were down. She'd had to photograph each page using her cell. When she got home later, she would send those photos like a fax to her boss along with her spreadsheet. If she could manage that before collapsing into bed.

# Excerpt from Bound by Air

Troy Waman looked down at his smartphone to the little red arrow blinking on his map app, indicating he had reached his destination. He frowned pensively before shaking his head.

"What a fucking shithole," he murmured to himself as he exited the nondescript black SUV his Station Master, Rex, had given him for the job.

*"Try not to scratch it,"* the tough Bear shifter had said with a barely contained growl after their meeting the day before last. After a thousand years of waiting, The *Wardens of Terra* were being called to duty and this was Troy's first assignment.

It took him a day and a half to make his way to Shadowland, New York from the little suburb in Virginia Beach where his Station was located. There were dozens of them across the continental United States and even more overseas, though he'd rarely been out of the county himself.

Troy rolled his shoulders and exhaled. He was the first from his Station to be called to duty. A fact that left him both proud and humbled at the same time. He'd trained damn hard since he was a child waiting for such an opportunity. Now he had it, and it was almost too much to bear.

*Fuck and damn. It's time Troy, get your ass in gear.* That was all the sympathy he had for himself. Why the hell should he have any at all? Troy Waman was no tenderfoot normal. He was a Warden of Terra. He didn't need to remind himself of the honor and duty that went along with his position.

The *Wardens of Terra* were an ancient group of elite warriors. All of them Shifters. Identified in their youth and trained throughout their preternaturally long lives, they were guardians as well as fighters. *Station Masters* led teams of Wardens across the planet.

Though they'd been deactivated sometime in the last millennium, Wardens were born, chosen, and trained every day with the distinct knowledge that someday, they'd be called upon to defend the earth. That day was here.

Troy Waman had been trained as a Warden since before he learned how to spell the word. His heritage was a mix of Anglo and Native American. His father's blood was a mix of tribes including Algonquin, Lenape, Cherokee, and a few others. He hadn't stuck around long enough for anyone to learn the rest.

He supposed he could get a DNA test, but that might raise too many questions with the normals. Especially in this day of advanced technology in biogenetics.

Besides, it was quite common in today's world to find Native American peoples descended from multiple tribes. Troy Waman was uncommon for an entirely different reason. He was a Shifter, a special race of dual natured beings with one foot in the supernatural world and one in the human. Troy was a *Thunderbird Shifter* to be exact. Something unique even amongst Shifters.

He stretched his long, lithe body as he stepped away from the vehicle. It was already dark out despite it being fairly early in the evening. *Daylight savings my ass.* He sniffed the frigid air. The unusually high winds made the cold seem even more bitter. The street lamp stuttered on the corner, a rusty fence squeaked, and a black cat crossed the street, ducking under some parked cars. Troy's frown deepened.

It looked like the setting of a B-horror flick. All it needed was some half naked co-ed to run down the street with a masked bogeyman stalking behind her, traditional blood-coated knife in hand. *Oh yeah.* They might call it *Shadowland Nightmare* or something equally cheesy.

He stopped his musings and used his heightened senses to take in the downtrodden area around him. It would seem upstate New York wasn't all orchards and sprawling suburbs. He smirked as the "I love New York" song ran through his head. *Yeah, right.*

Apparently, parts of the Empire State were as fucked up as the street where he was born in Newark, New Jersey. He'd visited that shithole back when he was in his teens just out of curiosity. What a mistake that had been! He'd left almost as soon as he'd arrived. His extended family had been, shall we say, less than welcoming.

His gray-haired grandmother had screamed and crossed herself when he stepped over her threshold. He was what they called a *skin walker*. They feared and loathed him as something evil. Him evil? Like he was the motherfucker who knocked-up some unsuspecting normal and left her ass with a Shifter baby.

He was not evil, but he was something they did not understand. He'd been angry and ashamed that day. He'd crashed through his grandmother's kitchen to hitch a ride back down to his Station in Virginia Beach.

In his youth it was more like a military training camp, but it was all he knew of home. After all, it was where he'd lived his entire life. He'd made his peace and settled fully into his life there.

The incident with his grandmother had happened over a decade ago, when Troy had stolen his records out of Rex's office. Still, the memory remained fresh in his mind as if it were only yesterday. The fucked-up street where he was standing only brought back the painful reminder that he'd come from the same kind of squalor. *Fuck this*, he thought.

The pungent scent of despair washed over him. *Reminding him.* A young man with a hood pulled up over his head, eyed him from the street corner. *Drug dealer. Shadowland* indeed. It was an apt name for this shamble of a neighborhood.

The young man continued to stare until Troy allowed his beast to shine through. His golden eyes pinned the errant youth through the inky darkness of the night. Startled, the kid dropped the bag he was holding and ran down the alley.

*Punk.* Troy walked over and picked up what he had so hastily left behind. A couple of grams of crack cocaine and heroin, *probably cut with Fentanyl.* There were also various sized baggies full of what smelled like some below average marijuana and half-rotted psychedelic mushrooms.

Just your garden variety of illegal substances to be found on most street corners in neighborhoods like this one. *Fucking normals.* He frowned and dumped the still sealed contents down the closest storm drain. He sent a quick text to Rex earmarking the location.

Rex would make sure the local police department got an anonymous tip to retrieve the narcotics before someone got hurt. Recreational drug use, mainly the opioid epidemic, was wreaking havoc amongst the humans with more and more of them succumbing to their addictions.

It was troubling, but not Troy's problem. Shifters were extraordinarily hard to kill. Most human drugs had little to no effect on supernatural beings. *Normals,* he growled the thought, *such weak creatures.*

To be fair, Shifters had vices too. He just had little

experience with it. Cecil, a Station-mate of his, had an adrenaline addiction. He was always putting himself in dangerous situations, even during simple training exercises. Fernandez, a Jaguar Shifter, was always trying to get into some chick's pants. *Sex addict.* And he knew of others who channeled their energies into ways he considered to be mostly unproductive.

His opinion, for sure. He'd always been something of a loner by nature. There weren't many Thunderbird Shifters around. Hell, he was the only fucking one he knew of in this part of the world.

He didn't blame or judge his Station-mates for their proclivities. Most of the Shifters he knew had large appetites which included food, exercise, and sex.

Troy had certainly explored that part of him. He wasn't a man-whore or anything, but he'd had his share of women. None of them mattered to him. Just a means to satisfy the occasional itch.

Troy was determined to live his life as a Warden of Terra alone. He never expected to find anyone willing to share what was a potentially deadly existence.

Those who followed the Darkness and evil were always looking for ways to gain the upper hand and it was his job to stop them. The way he saw it, it was an honor and a duty to serve.

He shared this great responsibility with the entire organization. The core belief of the Wardens was based on one indisputable fact Shifters had walked the earth since the dawn of time, even before humankind; therefore, they were responsible for the well-being of the entire planet and all its inhabitants. Especially those who were inherently weaker. Mainly females and *normals*.

There were other supernaturals who believed humans, or normals as they referred to them, were a blight on the planet. Those creatures wished to destroy them and take over.

Demons, Dark Witches, and a whole plethora of evil beings sought the destruction of the normals and the world they lived in. *Idiots! Did they even realize if they destroyed the world, there would be nothing left? Where the fuck would they live?*

Of course, the supernatural world had many agencies that worked towards the common goal of saving the planet. The *Order of the Guardians,* for example, were responsible for policing the various factions of supernaturals.

Shifters generally tended to ally themselves with the Guardians. Sure, there were *bad* Shifters, but he'd never come across any willing to follow the Dark. Simply because most agreed the destruction of the world could not be allowed to happen.

Different Packs and Clans, etcetera, of course, had different ideas. Some wanted to remain secret, others wished to come out, and other still wanted to rule the weaker humans. It was a whole fucking thing, and they argued about regularly.

Troy didn't know from any of that. He spent little time in the human world. His efforts better spent making himself worthy of being a Warden. Training, exercise, and following orders. That's what Troy lived for, it was why he was chosen.

Thunderbird Shifters were very rare. *Special.* He scoffed at the stray thought. But no matter what way he looked at it, Troy was indeed unique. In more ways than one. He was born *marked* by the stars. A *Shifter of Terra.*

From infancy, he was told he carried the power of his sign within him. *Aquarius* ruled his destiny and it would aid him in the never-ending battle against the forces of darkness.

Every single Warden he knew was a Shifter like him. They were the fiercest warriors on the planet. Like many others throughout the last thousand years, Troy, *a Shifter child who was marked,* was taken from his parents and trained by his Station Master until the time when he would be called into use.

*All that time,* he thought, *and here I am.* He tried to ignore the pressure building inside of him. He felt anxious. His animal pressed against his psyche, comforting him with his presence.

The significance of the moment was not lost on him. The Wardens had waited a millennium to be called to act. *He* had been waiting his entire life.

*"Do not fear the future, Troy,"* the Herald who had visited his Station said to him when he'd brought word that they had been activated, *"Your destiny awaits."*

Troy wondered if the old man referred to the Wardens finally being called to act, or if the elder spoke of yet another legend. Troy had been shocked to say the least when the Herald had entered their tidy little Station in Virginia Beach with his flowing white hair. After he told them the news, he turned to Troy and recited another old tale.

*"Young Thunderbird, you are the first to return us to Terra. Do not doubt your worth. Your destiny has been written in the stars since before you were born, Troy Waman. Remember, a Warden discovers his true measure when his fated mate is thrust upon him."*

*Whatever the fuck that meant.* Troy looked down at

his phone, then to the street sign on the corner, and finally, to the faded numbers painted on the mailbox in front of the ramble of a house his map app had brought him to.

*Fuck, am I thinking? Fated mates are myths.* Stories made up so orphaned Shifters would sleep through the night. He scoffed at the thought. Memories of tales the head nurse, Sr. Maria, had told him at the training camp he'd called home for years invaded his brain.

Memories were pesky things. Sometimes eternal, and always fucking portable. But he was no longer a child. *No more stories, Sister. Now, I act.*

"A thousand years we've waited, and I'm walking into a fucking scene from a bad episode of *Hoarders*," Troy shook his head and frowned at the decrepit house that sat a few hundred feet away from him.

It was cold as fuck outside and his leather jacket did little to warm him. Avian Shifters did not carry around the same bulk as other types of Shifters. He ran hotter than normals, but the single digit temperature froze him to the bone.

True, he wasn't beefy like some of his fellow Shifters, but he was just as incredibly strong, and he was wicked fast. Much stronger than any average male. He paused briefly gauging the atmosphere.

There was something off about the place. He scented *Magic* and something else. His Bird bristled beneath his skin. *Easy now.*

Lightning flashed in the darkened skies, allowing him to see the worn shingles, and cracked siding of the beaten-up colonial in greater detail. More than one window had been smashed and boarded up with cheap plywood.

If anything, it enhanced the creepy haunted house feel of the place. The porch sagged danger-ously. He wondered how the place had managed to not be condemned by the town. One thing was certain, it was an ugly little turd of a house.

*Who the hell put gray siding on their house anyway?* Maybe it wasn't always that color. Maybe the owner liked gray. *Whatever.* He couldn't give two shits about the siding.

His only concern was the increased supernatural activity in the area over the past two weeks. Ever since the owner, a *Mrs. Renalda Curosi*, passed away. *A haunting?*

A creaking sound floated up to his ears and he stilled his movements. The sound developed into more of a *moaning* noise. An unearthly wail. It grew louder as the lightning continued to flash in the sky.

Troy had never seen a ghost. True, there were a

lot of things in the universe he had never seen nor heard of, but that didn't make them any less real.

If ghosts were real, and they made noises, he imagined that pitiful wail was damn close to what it would sound like.

*No such thing as ghosts.* Yeah, well, most people had never heard of Shifters either. And yet, there he stood.

His Thunderbird shifted once more beneath his skin, the beast flexing his senses as the lightning in the air drew him to the surface. *No.* He told his other half. His human needed to be in control now. He walked across the street, keeping to the shadows.

Something was indeed off about the creepy old house. He inched further to the black door. The knocker was in the shape of a face or mask. No discernible features, just a vague impression of eyes, nose, and mouth. *Shadowland indeed.*

He listened with his enhanced hearing and frowned. There was a distinct voice somewhere beneath the moaning and creaking. A *female* voice. His curiosity was piqued.

From what he'd seen in her file, Mrs. Curosi was ninety-seven when she passed. Her closest living relative was a half-sister, a *Magdelena Kristos*, and she lived over three hours away in New Jersey. The half-sister was cut from Mrs. Curosi's will recently. She'd bequeathed her entire estate, house, bank account, and all her earthly belongings, to someone named *A. Kristos. Another sister? Maybe.*

Troy hadn't given it much thought until now. A crash sounded from inside the house. He perked up as the feminine voice he'd thought he'd heard earlier screamed in pain. *Time to act.*

"Are you fuckin' with me?"

"No, Randall, I assure you I am not fuckin' with you," Rafe Maccon eased his immense frame back into his oversized, black leather chair and narrowed his ice blue eyes at his Third and one of his oldest friends. How long had he known the man sitting in front of him?

Randall had come to Maccon City when Rafe was about ten, he looked the same then as he did now. Tall at six foot three inches, muscular, and more than a little intimidating to the Wolves under him with his long beard and equally long dark brown hair.

Rafe, however, was the Alpha. He was more amused than intimidated by his surly friend.

"A vacation?! What the fuck am I gonna do on a vacation? Come on, Rafe, this is bullshit!"

The door to Rafe's private office flew open and in strolled a very happy, very pregnant Charley Maccon, Rafe's wife. The Alpha's eyes glowed as they landed on his positively glowing mate. She wore a long, flowy dress. The shade was a pale-yellow color that, Randall admitted to himself, looked damn good with her creamy complexion and curly dark hair.

Their Alpha Female was quite something. There wasn't a Wolf Guard in the place who wouldn't lay down his/her life for her.

"Well, maybe you should consider a vacation to be a relaxing experience, Randy," she dropped a kiss on Randall's cheek and walked past him, over to her husband whom she kissed full on the mouth.

The way his Alpha's eyes homed in on her when she opened the door was nothing compared to the hungry gaze that followed her across the room.

Randall had noticed it took a while for Rafe to get used to his mate's habit of greeting everyone with a kiss or hug. Wolves were protective of their mates, but Randall thought his Alpha was doing an exceedingly good job of hiding his tension. Werewolves did not share very well.

Charley; however, had stood firm. That was the

way she was raised, and she wasn't going to change for any, how had she put it? Neanderthal brow-beating husband, regardless of how cute his ass was!

Randall had no direct knowledge if the "cute ass" statement was true or not. And he didn't want to know. He liked Charley though, had from the beginning. He was musically inclined and often took to one of the common rooms to strum his guitar or play a few keys on the piano.

# About the Author

C.D. Gorri is a USA Today Bestselling author of steamy paranormal romance and urban fantasy. She is the creator of the Grazi Kelly Universe.

Join her mailing list here: https://www.cdgorri.com/newsletter

An avid reader with a profound love for books and literature, when she is not writing or taking care of her family, she can usually be found with a book or tablet in hand. C.D. lives in her home state of New Jersey where many of her characters or stories are based. Her tales are fast paced yet detailed with satisfying conclusions.

If you enjoy powerful heroines and loyal heroes who face relatable problems in supernatural settings, journey into the Grazi Kelly Universe today. You will find sassy, curvy heroines and sexy, love-driven heroes who find their HEAs between the pages. Werewolves, Bears, Dragons, Tigers, Witches, Romani, Lynxes, Foxes, Thunderbirds, Vampires, and many more Shifters and supernatural creatures dwell within her worlds. The most important thing is every mate in this universe is fated, loyal, and true lovers always get their happily ever afters.

Want to know how it all began? Enter the Grazi Kelly Universe with Wolf Moon: A Grazi Kelly Novel or pick up Charley's Christmas Wolf and dive into the Macconwood Pack Novel Series today.

For a complete list of C.D. Gorri's books visit her website here:

https://www.cdgorri.com/complete-book-list/

Thank you and happy reading!

del mare alla stella,
    C.D. Gorri

Follow C.D. Gorri here:
    http://www.cdgorri.com

https://www.facebook.com/Cdgorribooks
https://www.bookbub.com/authors/c-d-gorri
https://twitter.com/cgor22
https://instagram.com/cdgorri/
https://www.goodreads.com/cdgorri
https://www.tiktok.com/@cdgorriauthor

www.ingramcontent.com/pod-product-compliance
Lightning Source LLC
Chambersburg PA
CBHW071402200726
48294CB00002B/275